Grady leaned closer and closer, making Laurel's eyes widen and the air between them crackle with electricity.

It was an electricity he'd avoided his entire adult life out of duty, out of a healthy belief in the history of Carsons and Delaneys and Bent and destruction.

"You're a Carson," she whispered.

He stared at her for something like a full minute, and then he laughed.

He supposed he had two choices. He could let her go find out whatever information she'd hoped to find, and wash his hands of messing with her or her investigation.

Or he could do what he should have done fifteen years ago when he'd caught Laurel Delaney snooping around his room after a sleepover with his sister.

He cupped his hand around her neck and pulled her mouth to his.

WYOMING COWBOY JUSTICE

NICOLE HELM

For all the Intrigue readers who took a chance on a new Intrigue author last year. Thank you.

Recycling programs for this product may not exist in your area.

ISBN-13: 978-1-335-63948-6

Wyoming Cowboy Justice

This edition published by arrangement with Harlequin Books S.A.

For questions and comments about the quality of this book, please contact us at CustomerService@Harlequin.com.

Printed in U.S.A.

Nicole Helm grew up with her nose in a book and the dream of one day becoming a writer. Luckily, after a few failed career choices, she gets to follow that dream—writing down-to-earth contemporary romance and romantic suspense. From farmers to cowboys, Midwest to *the* West, Nicole writes stories about people finding themselves and finding love in the process. She lives in Missouri with her husband and two sons and dreams of someday owning a barn.

Books by Nicole Helm

Harlequin Intrigue

Carsons & Delaneys

Wyoming Cowboy Justice

Stone Cold Texas Ranger
Stone Cold Undercover Agent
Stone Cold Christmas Ranger

Harlequin Superromance

A Farmers' Market Story

All I Have
All I Am

Falling for the New Guy
Too Friendly to Date
Too Close to Resist

Visit the Author Profile page at Harlequin.com.

CAST OF CHARACTERS

Laurel Delaney—A sheriff's deputy and upstanding member of the Delaney family who is deeply suspicious of the Carsons and who believes in the law above all else.

Grady Carson—Owns Rightful Claim, the local bar. Hates the Delaneys, but agrees to work with Laurel to help keep his half brother out of trouble.

Clint Danvers—Grady's half brother, unwittingly mixed up in trouble with the local mining company.

Gracie Delaney—Bent's coroner. Laurel's cousin.

Ty Carson—Grady's cousin. Former army ranger. Now helps out at Rightful Claim.

Noah Carson—Grady's cousin. Ty's brother. Runs the Carson Ranch.

Vanessa Carson—Grady's sister. Town mechanic, also helps out at Rightful Claim. Used to be best friends with Laurel.

Jen Delaney—Laurel's twin sister. Hates Carsons, especially Ty.

Mr. Adams—An employee of the mining company covering up illegal practices.

Chapter One

Laurel Delaney surveyed the dead body in front of her with as much detachment as she could manage.

"Know him?" the deputy who'd first answered the call asked apologetically.

"We're distantly related. But who am I not related to in these parts?" Laurel managed a grim smile. Jason Delaney. Her third cousin or something. Dead in a cattle field from a gunshot wound to the chest, presumably.

"Rancher called it in."

Laurel nodded as she studied the body. It was only her second murder since she'd been hired by the county sheriff's department six years ago, and only her first murder in the detective bureau.

And yes, she was related to the victim. Unfortunately, she wasn't exaggerating about the number of Bent County residents she was related to. She'd known Jason in passing at best. A family reunion or funeral here or there, but that was all. He didn't live in Bent, his parents—second cousins, she thought, to her parents—weren't part of the main offshoot of Delaneys who ran Bent.

"We do have a lead," Deputy Hart offered.

"What's that?" Laurel asked, surveying the cattle field around them. This ranch, like pretty much everything in Bent County, Wyoming, was in the middle of nowhere. No highway traffic ran nearby, no businesses in the surrounding areas. Just fields and mountains in the distance. Pretty and isolated, and not the spot one would expect to find a murder victim.

"The rancher says Clint Danvers broke down in front of his place last night. Asked to use his phone. He's the only one who was around. Aside from the cows, of course."

Laurel frowned at Hart. "Clint Danvers is a teenager."

"One we've arrested more times than I can count."

"Had to be a Carson," she muttered, because no matter that Clint wasn't technically a Carson, his mother was the mother of a Carson as well. Which meant the Carson clan would count him as theirs, which would mean trouble with a Delaney investigating.

Laurel herself didn't care about the Delaney-Carson feud that so many people in town loved to bring up time and again, Carsons most especially. Her father could intone about the generations of "bad element" that had been bred into the Carsons, her brother who still lived in Bent could sneer his nose at every Carson who walked into his bank, her sister could snidely comment every time one of them bought something from the Delaney General Store. The street could divide itself—Delaney establishments on one side, Carson on the other.

Laurel didn't care—it was all silliness and history as far as she was concerned. She was after the truth, not a way to make some century-old feud worse.

A vehicle approached and Laurel shaded her eyes against the early-morning sun.

"Coroner," Hart said.

Laurel waved at the coroner, Gracie Delaney, her first cousin, because yes, relations all over the dang place.

Gracie stepped through the tape and barbed wire fence easily, and then surveyed the body. "Name?"

"Jason Delaney."

Gracie's eyebrows furrowed. "Is it bad I have no idea how we're related to him?"

Laurel sighed. "If it is, we're in the same boat." It was a very strange thing to work the death of someone you were related to, but didn't know. Laurel figured she was supposed to feel some kind of sympathy, and she did, but not in any different way than she did on any other death she worked.

"All right. I'll take my pictures, then I'll get in touch with next of kin," Gracie said.

Hart and Gracie discussed details while Laurel studied the area around the body. There wasn't much to go on, and until cows learned how to talk, she had zero possible witnesses.

Except Clint Danvers.

She didn't mind arresting a Carson every now and again no matter what hubbub it raised about the feud nonsense, but murder was going to cause a lot more than a hubbub. Especially the murder of a Delaney.

She processed the crime scene with Hart and Gracie. Even though Hart had taken pictures when he'd first arrived, Laurel took a few more. They canvased the scene again, finding not one shred of evidence to go on.

Which meant Clint was her only hope, and what a complicated hope that was.

Gracie loaded up the body with Hart's help, and Laurel tossed her gear back into her car. "I'm going to go question Clint. You on until three?"

Hart nodded. "Let me know what I can do."

Laurel waved a goodbye and got into her car. She didn't have to look up Clint's residence as Bent was small and intimate, and secrets weren't much of ones for long. He lived with his mother in a falling-down house on the outskirts of Bent.

When Chasity Haskins-Carson-Danvers and so on answered the door, freshly lit cigarette hanging out of her mouth, Laurel knew this wasn't going to go well.

"Mrs. Danvers."

Chasity blew the smoke right in Laurel's face. "Ms. Pig," she returned conversationally.

"I'm looking for Clint."

"You people always are."

"It's incredibly important I'm able to talk to Clint, and soon. This is far more serious than drugs or speeding, and I'm only looking to help."

"Delaneys are never looking to help," the older woman replied. She shrugged negligently. "He's not here. Haven't seen him for two or three days."

Laurel managed a thin-lipped smile. It could be a lie, but it could also be the truth. That was the problem with most of the Carsons. You just never knew when they were being honest and helpful, or a pack of liars trying to make a Delaney's life difficult. Because to them the feud wasn't history, it was a living, breathing entity to wrap their lives around.

Laurel thanked Mrs. Danvers anyway and then sighed as she got back in her unmarked car. Most unfortunately, she knew exactly who would know where Clint was. And he was the absolute last man she wanted to speak to.

Grady Carson. Clint's older half brother and something like the de facto leader of the Carson clan. Much like the men in her family, Grady Carson put far too much stock in a *feud* for this being the twenty-first century.

A feud over land and cattle and things that had happened over a hundred years ago. Laurel didn't understand why people clung to it, but that didn't mean she actively *liked* any of the Carsons. Not when they routinely tried to make it hard for her to do her job.

Which was the second problem with Grady. He ran Rightful Claim, which she pulled up across the street from.

She glared at the offensive sign outside the bar—a neon centaur-like creature, half horse, half very busty woman, a blinking sack of gold hanging off her saddle. Aside from the neon signs, it looked like every saloon in every Western movie or TV show she'd ever seen. Wood siding and a walk in front of it, a ramshackle overhang, hand-painted signs with the mileage, and arrows to the nearest cities, all hundreds of miles away.

Laurel refused to call it a saloon. It was a bar. Seedy. It would be mostly empty on a Tuesday afternoon, but come evening it would be full of people she'd probably arrested. And Carsons everywhere.

Grady wasn't going to hand over Clint's whereabouts, Laurel knew that, but she had to try to convince him she only wanted to help. Grady was a lot of things—a tattooed, snarling, no-respect-for-authority hooligan—but much like the Delaneys, the Carsons were all about family.

Mentally steeling herself for what would likely amount to a verbal sparring match, Laurel took her first step toward the stupid swinging doors Grady claimed were original to the saloon. Laurel maintained that he bought it off the internet from some lame Hollywood set. Mainly because he got furious when she did.

She blew out a breath and tried to blow out her frustration with it. Yes, Grady had always rubbed her completely the wrong way, and yes, that meant sometimes she couldn't keep her cool and sniped right back at him. But she could handle this. She had a case to investigate.

Laurel nudged the swinging saloon doors and slid through the opening, making as little disturbance as possible. The less time Grady had to prepare for her arrival, the more chance she had of getting some sensible words in before he started doing that…thing.

"I see you finally found the balls to step inside, princess."

Laurel gritted her teeth and turned to the sound of Grady's low, easy voice. Doing that… thing already. The thing where he said obnoxious stuff, called her princess, or worse—deputy princess—and some tiny foreign part of her did that other thing she refused to name or acknowledge.

Her eyes had to adjust from sunlight to the dim bar interior, but when they did, she almost wished they hadn't.

He was standing on a chair, hammering a nail into the rough-hewn wood planks that made up the walls of the main area. Lining the doorway were pictures of the place over the years—a dingy black-and-white photograph of the bar in the 1800s, a bright pop of boisterous color from the time a famous singer had visited in the sixties, and photos documenting all Grady had done inside to somehow make it look less like a dive bar in a small town and more like a mix between old and new.

Much like the man himself. Laurel always had the sneaking suspicion Grady and the Carson cousins he routinely hung around with could straddle the lines of centuries quite easily. Sure, he was dressed in modern-day jeans and a simple black T-shirt that she had no doubt was sized with the express purpose of showing off the muscles of his arms and shoulders along with the lick of tattoos that spiraled out from the cuff and toward his elbow.

But he, and all the Carsons she had pulled over or served a warrant on more times than she could count on two hands and two feet, wore old battered cowboy hats like they were just dreaming of a day they could rob a stagecoach and escape to a brothel.

She wouldn't put it past Grady to *have* a brothel, but for the time being the worst thing he did in Rightful Claim was sell moonshine without a license.

Something she'd reported him on. Twice.

"Gonna stand there and watch me work all day? Want to slap my wrist over some made-up infraction?"

"It's funny you call this work, Carson. You don't have a single patron in here." She glared at the picture he rested on the nail he'd just pounded into the wall. It was a cross-stitched, nearly naked woman. Cross-stitched. Oh, she *hated* this place.

"There are no patrons because I don't officially open until three. But there's nothing like a Delaney coming into *my* place of business and criticizing *my* work ethic when your family has—"

"Please spare me the trip down family feud lane. I have business to discuss with you. It's important."

"*You* have business to discuss with *me*?" He got off the chair, just an easy step down with those long, powerful legs of his. Not that she noticed long or powerful, even when he was roaring his way down Main Street on that stupid, *stupid* motorcycle of his.

"I'm going to need a drink to go with this interesting turn of events," he drawled.

"You're going to drink before three in the afternoon on a day you're working?"

He walked past her, way closer than he needed to, and that wolfish smile was way too bright, way too feral. How could anyone call him attractive? He was downright…downright…*wild, uncivilized, lawless.*

All terrible things. Or so she told herself as often as she could manage to make her brain function when he was smirking at her.

"That's exactly what I'm going to do, princess."

"Deputy. This is official." She followed him toward the long, worn bar. Again, Grady claimed it was original, and it looked it. Scarred and nicked, though waxed enough that it shone. She couldn't imagine how anyone balanced a glass of anything on the uneven wood, or why they'd want to.

"All right, deputy princess—"

She was trying very hard not to let her irritation show, but the little growl that escaped her mouth whether she wanted it to or not gave her away.

The bastard laughed.

Low, rumbly. She could feel that rumble vibrate through her limbs even though there was this ancient big slab of a bar between them. *Hate, hate, hate.*

"Gonna report me again?"

She schooled her features in what she hoped was a semblance of professionalism. "Not this afternoon, though if I see you serve the moonshine when I know you don't have a license for it, I will contact the proper authorities."

"If that's your idea of pillow talk—"

"I know, all those multisyllable words, too hard for you to comprehend," she snapped, irritated with herself, as always, for letting him get to her. "But this is about your brother. And murder." His eyes went as hard as his expression, which gave her a little burst of satisfaction. *Not so tough now, are you?* “Care to shut up and listen?”

GRADY HAD ALWAYS had a little too much fun riling up the Delaneys, Laurel in particular. She got so pinched-looking, and when he really got her going, the hints of gold in her dark eyes switched to flame. And unlike the rest of the Delaneys, Laurel gave as good as she got.

But her words erased any good humor riling her up had created. Murder and Clint. Damn. Clint might be his half brother without an ounce of Carson blood in him, but he was still family. Which meant he was under Grady’s protection.

Grady jerked his chin toward the back of the bar. Though the regulars knew not to swing through the old saloon doors until three on the dot or later, he didn’t want anyone accidentally overhearing this conversation.

“I’m sorry, I don’t speak caveman. Is that little chin jerk supposed to mean something?”

He flicked a glance down her tall, slender frame. He could see her weapon outlined under the shapeless polo shirt she wore. The mannish khakis were slightly better than the polo because they at least gave the impression of her having an ass. A shame of an outfit, all in all.

"Let me ask you this," he said, leaning his elbows on the freshly waxed surface of the bar. He'd spent most of a lifetime learning how to appear completely unaffected when affected was exactly what he was, and this was no different. "Is this visit personal or professional?" he asked, making sure to drawl the word *personal* and infuse it with plenty of added meaning.

"Professional," she all but spat. "Like I said earlier. Trust me when I say I will never set foot through those pointless swinging doors for anything other than strictly professional business."

"Aw, sweetheart, don't lay down a challenge you won't be able to win."

"I see that even when it comes to your brother, you can't take anything important seriously. How about this? The murder victim is Jason Delaney. The only person around at the time of the murder was Clint Danvers."

Grady swore.

"I need to question your brother before news of this murder and that *he was a witness* spreads through town like wildfire. All we need is for one person to see a Delaney's been murdered, and know Clint is technically a Carson and a witness, and we have a whole feud situation on our hands. Are you going to help me or not?" she said evenly, the only show of temper at this point in her eyes, where he could all but picture the flecks of gold bursting into flame one by one.

He didn't trust a Delaney in the least, but Laurel Delaney wasn't quite like the rest. She hated the feud, and he almost believed she might be more interested in the truth than crucifying Clint without evidence. The rest of the town would be a different matter. This would result in the kind of uproar that could only cause problems for *everyone.*

Clint was in trouble, and Bent was in trouble, and the thing that kept the Carsons and Delaneys in this town, most of them hating and blaming each other for good or for bad, was that something about Bent had been poured into their blood at birth.

Something about the buildings that had stood the test of time in the shadow of distant, rolling mountains, far away from any kind of typical civilization. Something about the way history was imprinted into their fingerprints and their names, even if some people chose to ignore it.

Bent was like an organ in the body of those who stayed, and no matter what side of the feud you were on, Bent was the common good. Usually no one could agree on what that meant.

This wouldn't be any different. Laurel would want to solve the problem with warrants and investigations and all sorts of time-consuming bull. He and his cousins could have it sorted out with a few well-timed threats, maybe some fists, probably within the week.

So, he smiled at Laurel, as genially as he could manage for a man who wasn't used to being genial at all. "Have to pass, princess. Guess you and your gun will have to do all the heavy lifting."

Her eyes narrowed. "Sometimes I can't decide if you think I'm stupid or if that's just you. This is real life, Grady, not the Wild West—especially your lame version of it. If you want to arrest a murderer, you have to conduct an investigation. If you want to save your brother from the possibility of not just being a suspect, but being convicted, you need to work with the police. This isn't about Delaney versus Carson. It's about right and wrong. Truth and justice."

"Guess we'll find out."

She shook her head. "Don't come crying to me when Clint is locked up."

"Don't let the doors slap that pretty little ass of yours on the way out. You might end up enjoying it."

"You know, I don't get to say this enough in a day. Screw you, Grady." She flipped him off as she sauntered out of the saloon. The doors didn't hit her on the way out, but that didn't stop him from watching her disappear.

He waited until she was completely gone, then watched the clock tick by another few minutes. Casually, he pulled out his phone, then gave one last glance at the doors that had gone completely still. As if he didn't have a care in the world, he sent off a text to his cousins.

We need a meeting.

Ty was the first to respond. Mine, cow, or woman?

Grady's mouth quirked at the code they'd developed as teens. *Mine* was property, because the Carsons had managed to eke out some of their own, even with the Delaney name stamped all over this town since the first Delaney bastards had screwed the first Carsons out of their rightful claim to land and gold. Because of that nasty start of things in Bent, the Carsons didn't let anybody mess with what was rightfully theirs.

Cow meant family, because the Carsons and the Delaneys of old had gone to great and sometimes disastrous lengths to protect their livestock around the turn of the twentieth century, and these days, going to great lengths to protect family was still a number one priority for the Carsons.

And *woman*...

Grady stared at where Laurel had gone. Well, she was a woman, and she was a pain. A cop. A Delaney.

Yeah, he had a woman problem, but it was one that he was going to ignore, and it would go away. So, he typed Cow into his phone before grabbing his keys and heading out the back.

Chapter Two

Laurel wasn't big on breaking rules or protocol, but considering she was currently investigating a murder, and Grady likely knew where the only potential witness/suspect was, following him was necessary.

It was, however, difficult to follow someone surreptitiously in Bent. There weren't any cars to hide behind, and the roads that crisscrossed in and out of town were surrounded by long, wide stretches of plains, the mountains a hazy promise in the distance.

Still, when Grady's motorcycle roared out of town toward the west, quickly followed by another motorcycle, Laurel was pretty sure she knew where the motorcycle parade of doom was headed. Which made her job a hell of a lot easier.

She gave them a few minutes, then drove out

of Bent in the direction of the Carson Ranch. Though Grady didn't live there full-time, everyone knew he routinely bunked out at the ranch Noah Carson ran.

Much like the Delaneys tended to congregate around their own ranch on the exact opposite side of town. As if the two ranches were facing off, Bent their no-man's-land in between.

Laurel sighed. This whole thing was going to make that no-man's-land erupt into a chaos they hadn't seen for decades, if she didn't get some information out of Clint, and soon. She'd been stupid to think Grady had half a brain and would grant her access.

But she wasn't stupid enough to give up, and she was too darn stubborn to let Bent get dragged into another foolish war. It might not be the Wild West anymore, but people—many of whom were far too armed for their own good—getting riled up and fighting was never a good thing.

Especially when she had a murder to solve.

Laurel parked her car at the curve in the road, the last place she couldn't be seen. She'd have to hike up the rest of the way and do her best to stay behind underbrush and land swells and whatever she could find. Hopefully the Carson clan would be too busy planning how to hide away Clint to look out the windows and see her.

She pocketed her keys, checked her weapon and set out into the brisk fall afternoon. She remembered to turn the sound on her cell and radio off as she walked, keeping her eyes on where the Carson spread would eventually come into view.

When it did, she paused. She might be the practical, methodical sort, but she never failed to take a moment or two to appreciate where she lived. The sky was a breathtaking blue, puffy white clouds drifting by on the early fall breeze. The grass and brush were a mix of browns and gold. Surrounded by the all-inspiring glory of the majestic peaks of the Wind River mountains and the rolling red hills was a cluster of buildings sitting in the middle of a broad golden field.

The Carson Ranch wasn't much like its Delaney counterpart. It was populated with sturdy, mostly Carson-built buildings. They'd preserved most of the original ranch house, making improvements and expanding only when necessary. Like the saloon, it was a bit like stepping back in time with a modern layer over top.

The Delaney Ranch, on the other hand, was sleek, modern and gleaming, thanks to Laurel's father. The only building on the entire spread that predated her father was the one Laurel used as home right now. A tiny cabin that had supposedly been her ancestor's original homestead, though modernized with plumbing and electricity and whatnot.

It would fit in well enough on the Carsons' land. Laurel frowned at that uncomfortable thought. Nothing about her or her life would fit in with this group of ne'er-do-wells.

She edged along the fence line, trying to stay out of sight from any windows. Two motorcycles were parked in front of the main house, and Laurel had to wonder if they'd come here because Clint was here, or if they'd chosen the place to have some kind of pseudo-planning meeting.

Laurel knew one thing: Grady wasn't as nonchalant as he'd pretended. She'd never known him to bow out of the bar this close to opening before.

Maybe Clint *was* here. She could go to the house, demand to see him and show the three Carson cousins she wasn't scared of them—not Grady and his swagger, not Noah and his quiet stoicism, and not Ty, who'd recently returned after having served years as an army ranger. They might be big, strong men, but she was a law enforcement agent, and she'd faced bigger, badder men than them.

It would set a good precedent to stare them down, to demand access or answers. The Carsons seemed to think they were above the law, especially if it was a Delaney trying to enforce it, and she didn't have to let that stand.

But she didn't see another intact vehicle anywhere, just a handful of rusting, tire-less old cars and trucks. If Clint was here, he'd either gotten here on foot or hidden his vehicle.

There were a ton of outbuildings. While the Carson boys sat inside and planned whatever they were planning, maybe she could find a clue in one of those.

She quickened her pace, making it into the stables first. There were four horses in stalls, huffing happily, and a surprising amount of tidiness inside for the lack of it out. She made her way to the empty stall toward the back. It could fit a motorcycle or—

"Hands up," a husky feminine voice commanded.

Laurel whirled at the sound, hand on the butt of her weapon, and then scowled. "Vanessa, do not point a gun at me."

"Got a warrant?" Vanessa Carson asked, holding an old-looking rifle pointed directly in Laurel's direction.

"Is that a musket?" Laurel asked incredulously, then shook her head. "Regardless, stop pointing it at me. That's an official order."

With a hefty sigh, Grady's sister lowered her rifle. Laurel felt the same thing she always felt when she looked at her former best friend. Regret, and a pang for a childhood before things had been poisoned by some stupid feud.

"Why are you sneaking around our stables?" Vanessa demanded.

"Official reasons."

Vanessa smirked and pulled her phone out of her pocket. She held it up to her ear. "Hey, Grady. I'm out in the stables. We've got an uninvited visitor."

Laurel threw her hands in the air, frustrated beyond belief. "When will you all realize I am *trying* to help you. Help Bent." It was all she'd ever wanted to do. Help Bent. Even people who hated her because of her last name knew *that* was true.

"Helping Bent usually translates to helping the Delaneys when it comes to your people, Laurel. Why should this be any different?"

Laurel had a million arguments for that. Even though she'd beat her head against that concrete wall time and time again, she had no compunction about doing it again now. But she saw something out of the corner of her eye.

Something that looked suspiciously like a skinny teenager running for the mountains.

Laurel didn't hesitate, didn't concern herself with Vanessa's *musket*, of all things, and most definitely didn't worry about the impending arrival of Grady.

She pushed past Vanessa and ran after the quickly disappearing figure. She ignored Vanessa's shouts and put all her concentration into running as fast as she could.

"Clint Danvers, stop right there," she yelled, gaining absolutely no ground on the kid, but not losing any, either. "Bent County Sheriff's Department, I am ordering you to stop!" She could threaten to shoot, of course, but that would cause more problems than it'd ever solve.

Clint darted behind a barn at the west edge of the property, and Laurel swore, because he could go a couple different directions hidden behind that barn and she wouldn't be able to see which one he chose.

Her lungs were burning, but she pushed her body as fast as it would go, cutting the corner around the barn close. Close enough she ran right into a hard wall of something that knocked her back and onto her butt.

She would have popped right back up, ignoring her throbbing nose and butt, but the hard object she'd run into was Grady himself. And now he was standing there, giving no indication he'd let her pass.

She glared up at him and his imposing arms folded over his chest. "I detest you," she said furiously, even knowing she should tamp down her temper and be a professional.

His all-too-full lips curved into one of those wolfish smiles. "My life is a success, then."

"He's getting away, and if you think that's going to go over well for him, you're sorely mistaken."

Grady jerked his chin toward the house.

"Ty's after him on his bike. We'll have him rounded up in a few."

"Oh," Laurel managed to say, blinking. That was not what she'd expected out of Grady. At all. She figured he'd purposefully stepped in her way so Clint could escape.

"But I'm not going to let you talk to him, princess." He held out his hand as if he was going to help her up.

She pushed herself to her feet. "*Let* me?" she muttered. As if he could *let* her do anything in her official capacity.

"But I am going to clean you up. I think you might have broken your nose."

She touched her fingers to her nose, surprised to find a sticky substance there. She'd been so angry, she hadn't even realized her nose was bleeding. "I could arrest you for assaulting an officer."

"Babe, you ran right into me. That's not assault. It's not watching where you're going."

She didn't screech or growl or pound her fists into his chest like she wanted to. No, she took a deep breath in and then out.

She had a job to do, and Grady Carson could break her nose, threaten her sanity, but he could not stand in her way.

GRADY DIDN'T LIKE the uncomfortable hitch in his chest at the sight of Laurel's face all bloody. It was her own damn fault she'd crashed into him. He'd heard her coming, of course, but he hadn't known she'd turn the corner at the same exact time he had.

At full speed.

She was entirely to blame, but somehow he felt guilty as he walked her back to the main house. "We'll clean you up, then you can be on your way."

"I'm just going to come back with a search warrant. Clint is the only potential witness in a *murder*, Grady. I can't stop going after him until he answers some questions."

He hated that she was using that reasonable, even-keeled cop tone with him when there was a trickle of blood slowly dripping down her chin.

"Ain't none of my business what you got to do, Deputy," he said as lazily as he could manage, even though he didn't feel lazy at all.

His teenage half brother was a dope, plain and simple. Grady didn't think Clint had actually killed anyone, but he had a bad feeling based on Clint's running away that Clint knew *something*. Considering Clint's mom had kicked Clint out of the house just last week and had lectured Grady on getting him sorted out, Grady could only feel pissed and more of that unwelcome guilt.

He hated feeling guilty. So, when Ty pulled up on his bike, alone, Grady cursed. "Where the hell is he?"

"I don't know, man. Disappeared."

"That's impossible."

Ty shrugged. "Noah took one of the horses to go search the trees. What the hell happened to her?" Ty asked, gesturing toward Laurel.

"Your cousin broke my nose," the infuriating woman stated.

Ty's eyebrows winged up.

"I did not break her nose. She ran into me at full speed and broke her own damn nose."

"Want me to go open the saloon for you?" Ty asked.

Grady nodded and fished his keys out of his pocket. He tossed them at Ty. "I'll be there soon."

"You don't have to do this," Laurel said as Ty rode off. "My nose isn't really broken. It's just bleeding. I can clean myself up in my car."

"How do you know it's not broken?"

She shrugged. She was a tall woman, but

narrow. Narrow shoulders, narrow hips. Her hair always pulled back in a bouncy brown ponytail. Her face always devoid of makeup. Her body always covered up. The complete opposite of his type.

Which was why he'd never quite understood why his gaze tended to linger on her when they happened to be in the same vicinity, or why he got such a kick out of pissing her the hell off, and always had, since she'd been a girl hanging around his sister back before Vanessa had decided Delaneys were evil incarnate.

But one thing he did know and always had known—no matter how fragile Laurel Delaney could look on the outside, she was as tough as nails when it came down to it.

"I've had my nose broken before," she retorted. "I know what it feels like."

"You?"

"Yes, me." She glared at him, all piss and vinegar and a special brand of spitfire unique to her. "Meth-head head-butted me once."

"A meth-head head-butted you and your father let you stay in police work?"

"You don't know what I did to the meth-head in return."

Hell. Bloodthirsty was such a turn-on, even

on a Delaney. Maybe especially on one. "Come inside so we can wash you up before you slink back to wherever you hid your car."

"I did not hide my car."

Grady raised an eyebrow at her and she returned his look with an arch one of her own.

"I parked it down the hill so I could have a nice, head-clearing walk." She smiled sweetly.

"Sure." Grady pushed the front door open and led her into the kitchen. "Sit." He pointed to a barstool situated under the kitchen counter.

He grabbed a washcloth and ran it under some warm water before walking around to her.

"I can clean it myself," she said, holding her hand out for the cloth.

Instead he did what he knew would piss her off. He gripped her chin and held her head still as he used the washcloth to wipe away the blood.

She sat there regally, not sniping at him or pushing him away, and he had to fight back a smile over the fact she had changed tactics with him.

He wiped the blood from her nose and where it had dripped down her chin. She was fair-skinned and her nose was faintly freckled. While most Delaneys reveled in the finer things, the more genteel side of life, and her elegant face sure fit all that, Laurel had never been one for elegance and pretty things.

"You sure it's not broken?" he asked, and he was close enough that the hair hanging around her face stirred.

"I'm sure." She stared at him with those golden-brown eyes and there wasn't an ounce of animosity hiding there. He couldn't help that his gaze dropped to her unpainted mouth.

Laurel had always been easy to resist, not because he'd never found her attractive, but because it only ever took him opening his mouth to rile her up enough to have her walk away. But she wasn't bristling like she usually did, and he figured that was all kinds of dangerous.

"I'm not out to get you," she said as sincerely as she'd ever said anything to him.

Her sincerity was good enough to break this particular spell. "You'll have to pardon my lack of belief, considering how many times your father has tried to get Rightful Claim shut down." He stepped away and tossed the cloth in the sink. He crossed his arms across his chest and frowned intimidatingly down at her.

"That doesn't have anything to do with me. Should I blame you for everything your father's ever done? Because I hear it's quite a list."

He wouldn't admit she had a fair point.

"Work with me, Grady," she implored, speaking to him for once like he was a person instead of a Carson. "For your brother's sake. For Bent's sake. Put everything that came before behind us for the sake of *this* case and this case alone. If Clint is innocent, I don't want to be the one who puts him away for murder. I don't want a real murderer to get away with something because of feud crap."

"Haven't you ever heard the old saying that those who fail to learn from history are doomed to repeat it?"

"Well, I don't think there's any chance of me falling in love with you and dying in some army-led Native American massacre, or you and all the Carsons going off to war and eradicating an entire generation. So we might just make it. Did I cover all the idiotic Delaney-Carson fairy tales?"

His mouth curved. "I don't know, the illegitimate Carson who married a Delaney as payback always struck my fancy."

"That poor woman died in childbirth."

"And thus the waters between Carson and Delaney never commingled."

"You're terrible."

"Don't you forget it, princess."

The door squeaked open and Noah entered, slapping his cowboy hat against his thigh so that dust puffed up. "Must have had some help. That boy isn't anywhere out there."

"I need a list of friends, places he might have gone, that sort of thing," Laurel said in her demanding cop way that got Grady's back up like few other things.

But she'd implored him to help, and while helping a Delaney was the first and biggest thing on his *Don't Ever Do* list, this was about Clint. It was about Bent. Much as he might enjoy the feud tales and riling up the Delaneys, he didn't actually want any trouble in town. Trouble wasn't good for business, and as much as he would never admit to anyone, a little too hard on his heart.

He loved the town like he loved his brother. He loved his saloon like he loved the graves of every Carson before him. He might not have sworn to protect this place like Laurel had, but he had the sneaking suspicion they both wanted the same thing.

Damn it all.

"Your best bets are Pauline Hugh or Fred Gaskill," Grady offered.

Laurel hopped off the barstool. "Hugh, Gaskill. Got it. And if he comes back here, call me. Or bring him to me. I only need to question him. The longer he runs, the worse this looks. Please let him know that."

Grady nodded and Noah did, too, and then Laurel was striding out of the house.

"So, we're working with a Delaney," Noah said as if he didn't quite believe it.

"That Delaney and *that* Delaney only. And only until we get a handle on what Clint's involvement is and how much we need to protect him."

Noah made one of his many noncommittal sounds that Grady usually found funny, but he wasn't much in a mood to find anything funny today. "What's that grunt supposed to mean?"

"Oh, nothing. You just seemed awfully cozy with Deputy Delaney there."

"At least I wasn't blushing in front of her."

Noah bristled. "I was not blushing."

"Just don't get any hooking up ideas of your

own." Which was the wrong thing to say. It was beyond irritating, since he always knew the right thing to say, or when to keep his mouth shut. Grady never gave too much away.

Noah's rare smile spread across his face. "You staking a claim, cousin?"

"No, I am not. We just have to be careful how we play this. I'm going to work now. Go shovel some manure or something."

"Oh, there's plenty right here to shovel up," Noah replied.

Grady flipped him off and headed out of the house. He took a second to stand on the porch and look at the blazing sun in the distance, the rolling red hills, the rocky outcroppings of this beautiful Wyoming world.

He definitely wasn't watching Laurel Delaney stride down the long gravel driveway, a woman on a mission.

A mission he was more than a little irritated to find he shared.

Chapter Three

Laurel fumbled with her phone to turn off the beeping alarm. She wanted desperately to hit Snooze, but there was too much to do.

She hadn't gotten home until well after midnight, after tracking down all the names the Carsons had given her yesterday. She'd questioned both teens, but neither one had been able to give her the faintest hint on Clint's whereabouts.

She yawned and stretched out in bed. Oh, she didn't believe any of the shifty teenagers, but she couldn't force them to tell her anything. Which meant today would be another long day of investigating. Even if she got ahold of Clint to question him, she wasn't hopeful she'd get anything out of him.

She didn't have time to find Clint *and* investigate a murder that would be common knowledge in Bent and the surrounding areas by now.

Murder. Who had *murdered* Jason Delaney?

She forced herself out of bed and walked from her small room to the tiny kitchen. It was a cold morning, but it would have to be a quick one. Coffee, shower, get on the road. No time to build a fire and enjoy the cozy fall silence.

She frowned at the odd sound interrupting said silence as she clicked her coffee maker on. Something like a rumble.

Or a motorcycle.

"Hell," she muttered. She could not argue with Grady before she had coffee. Before she even had time to get dressed. She looked down at the flannel pajamas. It could be worse—she could be wearing the ones with bacon and eggs on them, or more revealing ones.

But she wasn't wearing a bra and she very nearly blushed at the idea of being bra-less in the same room as Grady.

She jumped at the pounding on her door, which was silly when she knew it had been coming. But she hadn't expected it to all but shake her little cabin.

Well, no time to fix the pajama situation. Worse, no time to fix the no-coffee situation.

So she put her best frown in place and opened the door. “What do you—” But she stopped talking because it wasn’t just Grady.

Grady shoved Clint through the door before following, and for a few seconds Laurel could only stand there and stare. Grady had brought her the only potential witness and the main suspect all rolled up into one. He’d brought a Carson into Delaney territory.

Grady scowled at—she assumed—the naked shock on her face. “The sooner you question him, the sooner you can clear him. You said you know he didn’t do it, after all.”

“I didn’t say that,” Laurel returned, shaking herself out of her shock and going for a notebook and a pen.

“What do you mean you didn’t say that? Never mind, Clint. Let’s go.”

Laurel stepped in front of him, holding out a hand to stop him. Somehow that hand landed on his chest. Because even though it was something like thirty degrees outside considering the sun was just beginning to rise, he only had a leather jacket on, unzipped, so that her hand came into contact with the soft material of his T-shirt, covering the very not-soft expanse of his very broad chest.

She jerked her hand away and focused on her notebook. “Calm down,” she said, hoping *she* sounded calm. “I said I don’t *think* he did it. I’m only out for the truth, and if the truth is Clint’s nose is clean, I’ll make sure my investigation reflects that.” She lifted her chin and met his blazing blue gaze.

She’d never seen Grady this riled up before. He was more of the “annoy the crap out of people till they took a swing at him, then gleefully beat them to a pulp” type.

Which was why it didn’t surprise her in the least when he relaxed his shoulders and his gaze swept down her chest. “Nice jammies.”

She sidestepped him and gestured Clint to a seat at her small kitchen table. “Sit, Clint. I have a few simple questions for you. Now, right now, we don’t know what happened, so I need you to be honest and forthcoming, because the more we know, the quicker we can get to the bottom of this.”

Clint sat in the chair, slumping in it, looking everywhere but at her or Grady. “Sure. Whatever,” he muttered.

Laurel opened up to a clean page in her notebook and quickly jotted down Clint’s name, the date and time. She left out Grady’s presence, and she didn't have time to wonder about why. "Now, Mr. Jennings said you came to his door around ten asking to make a phone call. Is that true?"

Clint shrugged again, fidgeting and sighing heavily. "Guess so."

"And why did you go to Mr. Jennings's door?"

"Crap car broke down not far from that rancher's house. I walked up, asked to use his phone since mine was dead, and then my girl came and picked me up." He pulled at a thread on the cuff of his jacket. "I wasn't anywhere near that field."

"How did you know the dead body was in the field?" Grady growled before Laurel could voice the same question.

Clint opened his mouth, but no sound came out. Laurel had to close her eyes. The idiot kid couldn't even lie? Hell, she'd come up with one if Grady's furious blue gaze was on her like that.

"You promised me you were telling the truth," Grady said, leaning over the table and getting in Clint's face. "So help me God, Clint, you do not lie to me and get away with it."

"Gentlemen," Laurel said in her best peace-making tone, smiling encouragingly at Clint and then Grady. "Let's take a calming breath."

She was pretty sure Grady's calming breath included picturing breaking her neck, but he stood stock-still, fury and frustration radiating off him.

If she hadn't grown up in this town, if she hadn't fascinatedly watched against her will, her whole life, how the Carson clan worked, she might have been concerned.

But where the Delaneys were all cold silences and sharp words, the Carsons exploded. They acted, and it was oftentimes too much and foolish, but Laurel had never doubted it came from the same place her family's way of dealing came from.

Love. Family.

Grady was pissed and frustrated—not just because Clint was lying to him, but at the fact Clint was clearly in trouble and Grady couldn't fix it.

"Let's start from the beginning, Clint," Laurel said evenly and calmly. "With the truth this time."

"Why are you making me talk to a Delaney?" Clint demanded of Grady. "She's going to railroad me no matter what I say."

Grady's entire face looked hard as marble, and the way he had his impressive arms crossed over his chest, well, Laurel didn't think she'd mess with him the way Clint seemed to be doing.

Clint sighed heavily, slouching even further in the chair. "Okay, yeah, I saw the body."

"You…" Grady was clearly working very, very hard not to come unglued.

Laurel held up a hand, hoping it kept him quiet rather than riling him further. "And you didn't call the police because?"

"Because me plus a dead body was only going to make me a suspect. I'm not stupid. I know how you cops work. Maybe you got something on Grady or are getting naked with him, but you got nothing on me."

Laurel hated that a blush infused her cheeks. Naked with Grady? Ha. Ha ha ha. What a laugh. But somehow she couldn't stop thinking about how she didn't have a bra on under her pajamas.

Laurel managed to clear her throat and look condescendingly at Clint. "Would you like me to arrest you? Because I can."

Clint began to bluster, but Laurel continued on in her even tone, because she would not be upset by a couple Carsons in her cabin. "Or you can truthfully answer my questions and allow me to investigate this. And, if you had nothing to do with it, this questioning will be all there is to it."

"I stood up for you with your mom, kid. You screw that up, you're out of chances, and you know it."

Clint stared at the table, but clearly, whatever Grady was talking about got through to him. "The story's all true. I just broke down on the other side of the ranch. I was walking up to the door to see if I could make a call when I heard a shot. I thought it was…" He shook his head. "Well, anyway, it was dark. I didn't see anything. But I heard the shot, a thump like a guy fell over, and footsteps running away."

Laurel scribbled it all down, her heartbeat kicking up. This was something. A lead, no matter how tiny, and that was important. "That's all you heard?"

"Think so."

"Thinking isn't good enough," Grady sneered.

"All right. That's enough out of you." Laurel stood and began pushing Grady into her bedroom. "You are officially uninvited to this questioning. You just stay in here until I'm done."

She pushed him and pushed him until he was far enough in her room she could close the door. Which she did. On his mutinous face.

GRADY STARED AT the rough-hewn wood of the door and tried very hard to resist the urge to punch it.

What did Clint think he was doing? Noah had found Clint holed up in the stables early this morning and they'd all surrounded him and demanded to hear what he knew. To make a plan. To protect their kin.

In *that* moment Clint had said he hadn't seen anything, that he was the innocentest of bystanders. That was the only reason Grady had decided to throw Clint on his motorcycle and drive him to Laurel's place.

If Grady had known the kid had *seen* it? Witnessed the murder go down and walked away? He would have called any lawyer he could afford.

Instead… Grady swore angrily, pacing Laurel's tiny bedroom. His idiot brother had just made everything ten times worse and *in* the house of a Delaney. How the hell was Grady going to get Clint out of this one?

He took a deep breath. He had to curb his

temper, because getting angry wouldn't help Clint. He needed a cool head and a plan.

He took stock of the room around him. Neat. Tidy. The bed was unmade, but considering Laurel was still in her pajamas, maybe she hadn't had a chance. Deputy Delaney did not seem like the type to leave a mess lying around.

She had a tiny bed, all in all. Bigger than a twin, he supposed, but not by much. Which was when he knew the best way to find a sense of inner calm in order to formulate a plan. It was not to go out there and bang his head against a hardheaded moron teenager, but to irritate the hell out of Laurel Delaney while she beat *her* head against Clint's teenage woe-is-me.

Grady settled himself in the middle of Laurel's bed. Comfortable, he'd give her that. The sheets were nice, and the pillows firm and plump and a lot better than the ones he had back at his apartment above the saloon or his bedroom at the ranch.

He grinned to himself, imagining asking her about where she got her pillows. Her eyes would do the fire thing, and she'd probably fist her hands on those slim hips.

Hips that had been settled in this bed this morning. In those ridiculous flannel pajamas. Except, he didn't think she was wearing a bra under said pajamas, and he wouldn't mind seeing what Laurel looked like a little unwrapped.

As it was, he could smell her. Something floral and feminine and so unlike her usual asexual appearance he was a little tempted to get his nose in there and take a good sniff.

Which was insane and more than a little perplexing. He didn't care what a woman smelled like. Vanilla. Citrus. Nothing at all. It was all the same to him as long as they were warm, willing and up for anything.

Laurel Delaney would not be up for anything.

Yeah, couldn't let himself go down *that* particular road. At least, not unless he was making her blush while he did it.

The door opened. Laurel stood with her notebook and pen in hand, her mouth opening to say something that was no doubt important.

Then she saw him and fury flickered across her features like a thunderstorm sweeping through the valley. "Get out of my bed, Grady."

"You know, a woman has never ordered me

out of her bed before," he returned conversationally, crossing his ankles.

"There's a first time for everything. Your brother's answers are sufficient for now, but he needs to stay in town in case I have more questions, and it's very possible he'll still be considered a suspect if I can't find something more concrete. But I don't have enough on him to apply for warrants, so I suggest you do your darnedest to get through to him."

"Will do, Deputy."

"Now, if you aren't out of my bed and my room in ten seconds, so I can get dressed, I will get my weapon and shoot."

Grady folded his arms behind his head and flashed a grin at her. "Go ahead and get dressed. I don't mind."

She made a squeal of outrage, or maybe she was actually having an aneurysm. "You have got to be the most infuriating man alive."

"Part of my charm."

"I'll claim immunity."

"Oh, don't tempt me to test that when I'm in your bed, princess."

"Ten, nine, eight..." She began to count, looking at the ceiling, which he'd count as a bit of a victory, because if she wasn't glaring at him maybe she was at least having a few inappropriate thoughts about him in her bed.

He would have been more than happy to let that countdown run out, see what she did. Would she really pull her gun on him? He doubted it. But whatever fun he was about to have was completely ruined when he heard his motorcycle engine start.

Without him anywhere near it.

Grady swore and hopped off the bed so fast the bed screeched against the hard floorboards. He ran past Laurel and out the door of her pretty little cabin and yelled after Clint's retreating form.

"That little punk will rue the day he touched my bike."

"Rue the day, huh?"

Grady whipped around to glare at Laurel, who was leaning against her open doorway, looking more than a little smug.

"No one, and I mean no one, touches *my* bike."

"It appears he already did."

Clint had indeed, and he would soon find out what it meant to cross Grady Carson, half brother or no half brother.

"I'll get dressed and drive you into town.

Just wait for a few minutes," Laurel said, pushing off the doorway and stepping inside. Grady took a few steps toward the doorway, but Laurel lifted an eyebrow.

"Out here," she added. And for the second time this morning, she slammed a door in his face.

Chapter Four

Laurel hummed to herself as she poured her coffee into her thermos. Turned out watching Grady get the crap end of the annoyance stick was quite the morning pick-me-up.

Plus, now she had a lead. It wasn't much of one, all in all, but Clint hadn't heard any yelling. Just murmured voices, which Laurel could safely assume meant Jason knew his murderer. Knew him and agreed to meet him in a field in the middle of nowhere.

Which meant Jason had been more than likely into something shady. So, her investigation needed to start focusing on her deceased distant relative.

It was a relief, in some ways, that it might be personal or even professional rather than random. Random was harder to solve. Random was more dangerous.

But Jason had known who killed him, there was a trail to follow, and she'd do her job to follow it.

With renewed purpose, and the image of Grady nearly losing his crap firmly in mind, Laurel slipped on her coat, hefted her bag and grabbed her thermos before heading outside.

She frowned a little when Grady was nowhere to be seen. Had he decided to walk back into town? No skin off her nose and all that, but quite the long walk in the cold when he didn't have to.

She walked to her car parked on the side of the cabin, and that was when she saw him.

He stood with his back to her, clearly surveying the sprawl of Delaney buildings—houses, barns, stables. Shiny, glossy testaments to the wealth and success of the Delaney clan.

It shouldn't make her uncomfortable. Her family had worked long and hard for their success, *and* they'd always upheld the law while they did it. She was born of sheriffs and bankers and good, upstanding people. She *knew* that.

But no matter how traitorous the thought, she'd always been a little jealous of the Carsons. Not their wildness by any means, but the way they treated their history. They didn't just know the dates and the people, they lived it. Embodied it. A Carson today was not much different than a Carson one hundred years ago, she was sure.

Laurel had always felt a little disconnect at her father's edicts of bigger, better and more when they had so much to be proud of just in who they were.

"Tell me something, princess," Grady said, his voice something like soft. Which might have bothered her, or affected her, if she thought it was sincere. As it was, she figured he was just trying to lower her guard.

"What's that?"

He turned slowly, those blue eyes of his direct. Sometimes she wondered if she couldn't just see the past through them.

Get a hold of yourself, idiot.

"You don't believe in the feud," he said in that rusty scrape of a voice that might have made women weaker than her shiver. "So, what do you believe in?"

She didn't need to think about it, or even look away. "Bent."

He sighed heavily, his gaze traveling to the mountains in the distance. "I was afraid that's what you'd say," he muttered. "I suppose we don't agree about the way people go about it, but I feel the same. As long as Clint's a suspect, Bent's at risk."

"I agree."

"So, I'm going to help you."

Laurel frowned. "I don't need your help, Grady. This is my job."

"And if everything Clint says is true, that relative of yours was in some shady business that got him killed."

Laurel's frown deepened. She hated that he'd put that together, even if it was easy enough. Grady had good instincts, and she didn't want to have to compliment him on them. Or anything.

"And, baby, you don't know a thing about shady. But I do."

"What are you going to do? Eavesdrop at the bar? Beat a few answers out of people? This is a police investigation."

"I can be subtle."

She barked out a laugh. "You're as subtle as a Mack truck. One that nearly broke my nose."

Grady quirked one of those smiles that, if she wasn't careful, could make her believe there was some softness in this man. But that was utter insanity. Grady was and always had been the opposite of subtle or soft.

"I can listen. I can put out a few feelers. I can do it all without anyone raising an eyebrow. It's the beauty of owning a saloon."

"Bar," Laurel muttered. But she didn't get the rise out of Grady she expected.

"This is my brother we're talking about, Laurel."

Her first name. Not *princess*, not Delaney. Just her first name.

"Okay," she said carefully, because even though she knew she shouldn't let it get to her, it did. If the positions were reversed, if one of her siblings were in trouble… Well, she'd probably break a few laws. Who was she to think Grady couldn't uphold a few to save his brother? And Bent. "But you'd have to promise me, really, honestly promise, that we do this *my* way. If there's a murderer out there, I have to be able to build a case on him. One with evidence, and no questions as to the validity of that evidence. Or a *murderer* gets away." She refused to entertain that thought, but Grady had to.

His jaw tightened, but he didn't smile or

joke or do anything except nod. Then hold out his hand.

"You have my word."

Laurel could not have predicted this turn of events in a million years. Working with a Carson… It was insane, and risky, but maybe if the town saw a Carson and a Delaney working together for the truth, they'd be able to find something of the same.

She took his outstretched hand and shook, firmly. "So. We're in this together," she said, because she couldn't quite believe it.

"Only until my brother is cleared and to save Bent from another wave of feud crap."

"I thought you believed in the feud wholeheartedly."

"I believe in enemies. I believe in history. I believe in Delaneys mostly being so high on their horses they don't see anything."

Laurel tried to tug her hand away, but Grady held it in his, his large hand grasping hers tightly.

"I believe violence is *sometimes* the answer. Just like I can believe in the feud, the importance of that history, and think not *all* Delaneys are scum of the earth." His mouth curved into that dangerous thing. Dangerous and feral and so completely the opposite of arousing.

She wished.

"But mostly, Deputy Delaney," he said, holding firm on her hand and even tugging her closer. Close enough she could feel his breath mingle with hers, close enough she could see that the vibrant blue of his eyes matched the blue of the fall sky above them.

"I believe in Bent. And I believe you do, too. So, we'll do this your way until we have the murderer behind bars."

"And after that?"

"After that, I'll go back to doing things my way, princess." The curve of his mouth morphed into a full-blown grin. "So try not to fall in love with me."

"Such a hardship," she muttered, and when she gave one last tug of her hand and he didn't let go, she let her temper take over a little bit. She moved quick and clean and managed to land an elbow to his stomach that had his grasp loosening enough for her to free herself.

"Next time you hold on to me like that, you'll let me go the first time I pull away, or that elbow to the gut will be a knee to the balls."

Grady made a considering noise. "I like that

you plan on there being a next time I hold on to you like that. Desperate for another touch?"

"I don't know how you'll hear anything shady going on in that bar of yours over the infernal buzz of your outrageous ego."

"I think I'll manage."

And the irritating part was, she was quite positive he would.

GRADY HAD CONSIDERED, for a moment or two, hauling her over his shoulder as payment for the elbow to the gut. Maybe he'd even slap that pretty ass of hers for good measure. It was a fantasy with some merit, but it would have to stay a fantasy.

He'd heard enough bedtime stories about a one-hundred-and-fifty-year-old feud to know that Carsons and Delaneys getting mixed up in each other's asses was never, ever a good thing.

Besides, he needed to focus on Clint, which meant figuring out this case. A lot faster than the police would. He got that Laurel had some of the same concerns he did, and he got and respected the fact she knew what she was doing.

But he didn't have time for bureaucratic red tape, or following all leads. *His* goal wasn't so much the truth as it was making sure his brother didn't get wrapped up in this. Laurel could do her police work, focus on her job, and Grady could focus on Clint.

It made them something like the perfect team. Which made it something like amusing to follow her to her car and get in as a passenger. She tossed her bag in the back, and got into the driver's seat as he stretched out in the passenger's.

"Can't say I've ever sat in the front seat of a cop car before."

"And I've never been pushed into the back of one. Such different lives we've led," she returned dryly, turning the keys in the ignition.

She drove away from the Delaney spread, a monstrosity of glitter and shine, the antithesis of what it should be in Grady's estimation. You built a name for yourself, you ought to give some nod to the past platforms you built yourself on. But the Delaneys liked it slick and *new*. And if he was being honest, at least part of the appeal for the Carsons was finding joy in the old and patched-together.

"You guys really hire *all* your ranch work out?" Grady asked, more because he knew it would make her stiffen than because he didn't know.

"Dylan helps some. Cam might when he comes home. Being a navy SEAL keeps him busy."

Grady made a humming noise he knew would irritate her. "Seems a bit of a misnomer to call it the Delaney ranch, then."

"If you insist," she replied, and though she clearly tried to use cop tone on him, some of her snap crackled through.

Grady grinned. Laurel always gave a hell of a snap. "Where exactly are you planning on letting me out?"

"Rightful Claim," she replied matter-of-factly as she maneuvered her neat, sparkling car down the winding road back toward the town's heart.

"So, you're going to drive through town, for all and sundry to see, and then drop me off at my bar to do the walk of shame?"

Her head whipped to his for a brief second before she returned her concentration to the road. "No one will think that."

"Baby, *everyone* will think that. What better story is there in Bent? Number one: a Carson murdered a Delaney. Number two: a Carson defiled a Delaney. Hell, we could create our very own Civil War."

"That isn't funny."

"It wasn't a joke." Though he couldn't blame her exactly for thinking he took this lightly. He wasn't a man prone to giving away his deeper emotions. Especially to the Delaneys, but he was also no idiot. Once the whisper of murder made it through town and who the suspect was, added to any whisper of him and Laurel spending time together—no matter how ludicrous—things would really get going.

Any romance rumors now would only fan the fire, and make him and Laurel's life harder while they were trying to clear Clint.

Laurel sighed heavily. "So, where do you want me to drop you off?"

"Go out of town to the north, circle around back, and there's a small, gravel access road back of Carson property we can sneak through."

"I should not have to sneak. Or waste half my morning sneaking."

"Lotta things we shouldn't have to do in this life, princess, but we do them anyway."

Her lips firmed, but she posed no other arguments. Her dark hair was pulled back in a ponytail, as it usually was, her jaw clenched tight, also usual. But something about seeing her in her pajamas, lying in her bed—it was like seeing a slightly different, softer side to Laurel Delaney.

He clearly needed more coffee. He didn't needle her the rest of the way. Well, he fiddled with the buttons on her fancy police car dash, even in this unmarked car, before she slapped at him, but other than that he was on his best behavior.

He couldn't imagine Clint had ridden Grady's motorcycle anywhere else but the Carson ranch, because if the kid had, well… Grady wouldn't consider it on account of a bad temper and an insane dislike to people touching his few prized possessions. His bike chief among them.

Morning broke like a glorious blast, rays of sunshine reflecting the gold of everything. Fall in Bent could make the snobbiest of city folk smile. As for Grady, it was always a reminder his soul belonged here. Those roots that bound him to this land and that sky weren't shackles but gifts.

He glanced at Laurel. She did everything

efficiently. The turn of the wheel, the checking both ways before making a turn. Always so serious and conscientious. He supposed that was the fascination. He'd never known anyone quite like her, even in the passel of uppity, glossy Delaneys that ran Bent, or tried to.

"Turn here," Grady instructed, gesturing toward a barely visible turn off the highway. Laurel nodded and drove her car through a canopy of green and gold, leaves and pine, until they reached the gate.

"You can walk from here," she said primly.

Something about her prim always made him grin. "A polite woman drops her man off at the door."

"Consider me impolite and you very much not my man."

Grady pushed the car door open and stepped out. "I'll put a few feelers out tonight at Rightful Claim, let you know what I come up with."

She nodded, all business. "I'm going over to the mining company to talk to Jason's boss and any coworkers he might have been friendly with. I'll let you know if I've got a specific lead I want you to listen for."

"Look at that, Deputy, we're acting like partners already."

She rolled her eyes. "We'll be lucky if we don't kill each other."

The grin that had never fully evaporated spread across his face. "Funny, killing each other isn't what I'm worried about."

Her eyebrows drew together, all adorable, innocent confusion. Oh, to be as sweet and rule-abiding as his deputy princess.

"You just think on that, and we'll be in touch." He closed the door and started walking toward the old homestead. The wind was cold, but he didn't mind. It was a good kind of cold. A thinking cold. And he needed to get his head in the thinking game. The keeping-Clint-out-of-trouble game.

When Laurel's car didn't immediately turn around and drive away, he chuckled. He kept walking, but he waited for what he knew would come. Because deputy princess didn't know when to quit.

He supposed that was fair. Neither did he.

"I will never sleep with you, Grady Carson," she shouted through her open driver's side window.

He just raised a hand in salute. He didn't

think of "never" so much as a challenge as he considered it a curse. And there were already plenty of Carson and Delaney curses in the air.

Chapter Five

Evergreen Mining existed about thirty miles outside of Bent, and straddled Bent and Freemont counties with its sprawling compound in the middle of just about nowhere. Little boxlike things dotted the landscape as Laurel explained who she was and showed her badge to the security entrance.

Laurel didn't know much about the company. No one in her immediate family or group of friends worked this far outside of Bent. She did remember the mine here getting in trouble a few years back for some safety regulations, but she hardly expected her accountant victim to have been involved in any of that.

At best, she'd find a link to someone who might have wanted Jason dead. At worst, it was a dead end and she'd have to start prodding Jason's family. She sighed. She almost wished she knew that line of the family better, but as the son of her father's second cousins, they were so far removed she barely even heard gossip about Jason.

Laurel was led to the office of Jason's boss by a secretary. The secretary knocked on a door and then pushed it open, stepping inside and gesturing Laurel to follow. "Mr. Adams, the police are here to ask you a few questions."

"Yes. Of course." A well-dressed middle-aged man stood from behind a desk and held out his hand. "I'd be happy to assist you in whatever way I can, miss."

"Deputy Delaney," Laurel said, shaking his hand in return.

The man shook her hand, looking at her quizzically. "You're related to Jason?"

Laurel forced herself to smile. "Yes, though distantly."

"Ah. Well, have a seat. I'd be happy to answer any questions you may have. I do have an appointment with my foreman in twenty minutes that I can't miss." He smiled apologetically. "Regulations and all that."

"Of course. I mainly just need a list of anyone Jason had routine contact with, and if you know of anyone he might have had a disagreement with or dislike of."

"Well, our administrative staff is somewhat isolated out here, Miss Delaney."

Laurel bit back the need to correct him. *Deputy, not Miss, jerk.* "Did he have a secretary or an assistant?"

"No. Jason was a satellite accountant, meaning he kept track of our accounting at this plant alone. He would have answered to the head accountant in our main office in Nebraska."

Laurel continued to ask him questions, and Mr. Adams continued to give vague, unhelpful answers for twenty full minutes. Finally, Mr. Adams stood. "I have my meeting. Is there anything else—"

"I'd like access to Jason's things. Did he have an office?"

Mr. Adams frowned but quickly smoothed it out. "Follow me, miss."

Laurel scowled at Mr. Adams's back, but followed him back out into the hallway and down a few doors. Mr. Adams pulled out a key ring and unlocked the door.

"Feel free to look around as much as you'd like. If you need to take anything, I'm afraid

I'll have to approve it. Jason did have access to some sensitive documents."

"I'm sure copies can be made of anything that might aid me in my investigation." Laurel smiled brightly at him.

Mr. Adams smiled thinly. "Of course. If you can't find me, my secretary should be at her desk. She can also summon anyone else you may need to talk to. If you'll excuse me."

Laurel nodded and stepped into the office. It was small and cramped, and messy. She sighed. It was hard to find clues when you didn't know what you were looking for. Long, frustrating hours of sifting through crap. Her least favorite part of the job.

But it was part of her job, so she got to work. She didn't know how long she filtered through the papers on Jason's desk before she finally found something of potential interest. A scrap of paper in a file with the name Jennings scribbled on it.

Considering Jason had been found by a Mr. Jennings, that seemed incredibly pertinent. A quick scan of all the papers in the file gave Laurel no clue as to why, but with some closer reading, she might be able to find something.

The door swung open and a man entered,

stopping short. He was youngish. Maybe midtwenties, dressed like he didn't belong in the administrative building. Jeans, a heavy-duty jacket and heavy work boots.

"Who are you?" he demanded. "Where's Jason?"

Interesting. She supposed the appropriate thing would be to tell this man what had happened to Jason, but she wanted a little information first. Especially since Mr. Adams considered Jason so isolated.

"Hello. I'm sorry, who are you?"

The man frowned. "Jason get fired or something?"

"Actually..."

"You know what, never mind," the man mumbled and rushed out the door.

Very, very curious. Laurel clutched the file and hurried after him, trying to make her strides look relaxed.

He passed the secretary, busting out the door with a hard push.

Laurel stepped up to the secretary's desk. "Who was that man?"

The secretary didn't even look up. "Hank Gaskill."

Gaskill. Why did that sound familiar? Laurel pushed the file toward the woman, getting out her notebook and writing down the name. "Can I get copies of everything in this file?"

The secretary took the file and frowned. "This was in Jason's office?"

Laurel raised an eyebrow as she placed the notebook back in her pocket. "Yes."

"It shouldn't have been. This is Mr. Adams's file, and it doesn't have anything to do with accounting or finances."

A lead. A *real* lead, then. "Then I definitely need copies."

The secretary nodded and turned to a copy machine behind her.

"Does Hank Gaskill come to visit Mr. Delaney often?" Laurel asked.

The secretary shrugged. "Lately they've gone to lunch together. Childhood friends, from what I could tell."

Yet, Hank hadn't heard that Jason had been murdered. Interesting. "Thank you." Laurel got her card out of her pocket and handed it to the secretary. "If you or Mr. Adams or anyone thinks of anything else, please be sure to call me."

The secretary handed over the copies and

took Laurel's card. "I will. Jason was so young. Such a tragedy."

Laurel nodded and slipped the papers under her arm, heading back out to her car. *Gaskill. Gaskill.* Why was that familiar?

She walked to her car, turning over the events of yesterday in her mind, and that's when it dawned on her.

Fred Gaskill. Clint's friend she'd questioned yesterday.

Oh, damn that kid and his lies.

GRADY WAS IN a piss-poor mood as he opened Rightful Claim. He'd spent too much of his morning searching for Clint. The teen had, sensibly, left Grady's bike at the ranch, but had disappeared after that.

Grady had a saloon to run and things to do, and his half brother was putting a dent in both.

"I take it you don't have any ideas on how to bring him to heel," Ty asked, pulling chairs down off the tables. Since Ty had basically just gotten back to Bent after a stint as an army ranger, he was going to be working at the bar until he decided what he wanted to do next.

"I'm washing my hands of that kid," Grady muttered, putting cash in the register for the evening.

"Yeah, you're so good at washing your hands of people."

Grady only grunted. So, maybe giving up on people wasn't exactly his strong suit. But that was because he always did some good. If Clint didn't want some of that good, well, fine. Grady would let him off the proverbial hook.

Soon as he got Clint cleared of murder.

The saloon doors swung open and Laurel stepped into the dim light of the bar. She was dressed exactly as she had been this morning, except her weapon was strapped to her hip.

The fact his spirits lightened enough he could feel a weight lift in his chest was kind of worrying, but he'd wrap that up in sarcasm and irritating the crap out of her.

"She deigns to walk through our doors, Grady. To what do we owe the unwanted non-pleasure?"

Something about Ty giving her a hard time bothered him in a way he did not care for at all. "Watch the bar," Grady ordered gruffly.

He ignored the shock on Ty's face and jerked

his head toward the back. "Follow me," he said to Laurel.

She pressed her lips together, but didn't argue. So, instead of leading her to one of the back rooms or the kitchen or anything that might have been easy and safe, he led her upstairs to his apartment.

Her pressed-lips look had morphed into a full-blown scowl as he opened the door and gestured her inside.

"Do we really need to talk up here?"

"Private," Grady returned cheerfully. He entered the apartment and turned to give her an impatient look.

She huffed out a breath but stepped inside. She wrinkled her nose. "Your bedroom isn't even separate from your kitchen?"

"But the bathroom is separate, which is probably far more important." He nodded toward the bed that took up a considerable amount of space in his kitchen/living/bedroom area. "You want to lie down on my bed? Tit for tat and all that?"

"Gaskill," she said firmly, though he didn't miss the way her eyes drifted to his messy, unmade bed. "Fred Gaskill is friends with Clint, and claimed he didn't know anything about Clint's whereabouts."

"Yeah."

"Do you know anything about Hank Gaskill?"

"Fred's older brother. Works at the…mine." Which was where Laurel had been headed today.

"Friends with Jason. He popped into his office today while I was looking through Jason's things. Skittered off like he was afraid." Laurel frowned, a line digging into her forehead. "But he didn't seem to know Jason was dead."

"What does it mean?" What did it mean that one of Clint's friends had a brother who was friendly with a dead man? It could mean nothing in a small, rural county. A coincidence. But Grady wasn't sure he believed in those with a murder having gone down.

"I don't know. I've got some more digging to do, but—"

"What kind of digging?"

"Police digging. Does Hank ever come in here?"

Grady didn't care for the brush-off, but he didn't press it. Yet. "A handful of the mining guys do occasionally. Not much else in the way of a place to hang out and get a drink for those who live on this side of things."

"I need you to call me if they ever come in. Day or night. On duty or off. You call me."

"What? So you can oh so subtly eavesdrop?"

"Maybe."

Grady snorted. "Princess, everyone knows you don't come into Rightful Claim, and this is time number two in a week. Make it a third, especially during working hours, the whole town might implode with the implications of a Delaney in a Carson establishment."

"Carsons bank at Delaney Bank and shop at Delaney General all the time."

"It ain't the same, and you know that."

Laurel blew out an irritated breath. "Regardless. You call me. Something is off with everything I witnessed today. Hank coming into Jason's office, then files on his desk that shouldn't have been. I can't tell if the boss is just a patronizing, sexist douche or an actual criminal."

"Maybe even both."

She frowned. "He called me *miss*."

"So, if I really want to piss you off I should call you Miss Deputy Princess."

She rolled her eyes and made a move for the door, but Grady blocked it.

"Out of my way."

"What's the plan, Delaney?"

"The plan is for me to continue investigating per my job. If you see Hank *or* Fred Gaskill in your bar, or doing anything fishy, you call me."

"And that's it? My kid brother might be on the hook for murder and I'm just supposed to play lookout?"

Some of that pissed-off hard edge softened. "What else is there to do, Grady? I have due process to follow. You can't go with me to search Jason's place, and I can't hand over evidence. Both of our hands are tied."

"I really prefer to do the tying," he joked even though he didn't feel like joking in the least.

Laurel's gaze slid to the bed again before she seemed to shake herself out of it. "Regardless. I need you to sit tight and watch. I need you to have some patience."

Grady ran his palms over his beard. Hands-tied patience. When had he ever not balked at that? But no matter how many times he'd acted against all he'd been told to do, when he *acted* he did so knowing he was right.

The worst part of all this was knowing Laurel was right. He was no cop. He had no authority to arrest or try a murderer, and an eye for an eye wasn't going to work.

"You get really quiet when you know I'm right," she offered with a smirk.

The hands-tied frustration bubbling through him and that self-satisfied smirk of hers right next to his bed was the kind of terrible concoction that led to bad decisions.

Still, holding himself back in one arena meant holding himself back in another wasn't a possibility. So, he stepped forward, and when she lifted her chin to meet his gaze rather than step back, he grinned.

"Do I, now?" he asked quietly, reaching out and taking one of those flyaway strands of her hair between his fingers.

She kept that haughty expression on her face, but he watched her elegant throat move as she swallowed.

"You don't believe in the feud, but do you believe in the curse?"

"What curse?" she asked, clearly attempting nonchalance. But she didn't meet his gaze when she asked.

"The one that says if a Carson and a Delaney even look at each other with so much of an ounce of kindness, or *other* nice things, the whole world goes to hell. Just like my favorite illegitimate Carson and his Delaney bride who died, and the Delaney girl who would've married the Carson boy if not for World War II, and then there's your sis—"

That dark, irritated look returned. "There's no curse. I'm being nice to you, aren't I?"

He twisted her soft strand of hair in his fingers. "Could be nicer."

Her eyebrows furrowed, but she didn't pull away and he'd be damned if her gaze didn't drop to his mouth. But when she looked back into his eyes, there was something he didn't want to notice, even if he did.

A note of vulnerability to invulnerable Laurel Delaney. "What game are you playing, Grady? Because I'm not playing one."

"No games. Just..." He leaned a little closer. "Chemistry. Admit it. Does it hurt so very much to admit it?"

Laurel stared at him for a few humming seconds. Seconds he thought she might have actually considered *chemistry.*

But then she shook her head. "You're not

funny." She stepped around him, her hair sliding out of his fingers.

There were ways to stop her, sarcastic things to drawl her way, but he couldn't get over the fact she didn't seem so much irritated by him as something else. Something a lot softer.

Grady didn't poke at soft. He might be his father in a lot of ways, but not that one. "Listen." He turned to face her, frowning at the fact she already had the door open and was striding out of it. "I'll give you a call if anyone from the mine shows up."

She paused in his doorway and straightened her shoulders, but she didn't turn around. "Great. Thanks."

Then she was gone, and he was left in the same piss-poor mood he'd been in before she'd arrived.

Chapter Six

"This isn't going to work."

"Not with that attitude," Jen said to Laurel, all too cheerfully. "This was your idea. Don't start pooh-poohing it after all the work I've put in."

Laurel sat in her sister's tiny bathroom, second-guessing her plan. And then third-guessing it. Until the number got too high to count.

"I watched too many detective shows as a kid. It's infected my brain and this is a terrible idea," Laurel said dejectedly.

"No, the terrible idea is trusting Grady Carson."

"Don't start."

Jen handed Laurel a small mirror and Laurel studied her reflection. The wig didn't look ridiculous, and though she *felt* silly, Laurel knew that on the surface she looked like any normal twentysomething.

The problem was she'd *never* been a normal twentysomething. Her life since she could remember revolved around becoming and then being a cop. No parties, little dating. She didn't go to bars or flirt with guys. Ever.

Plus, she didn't think she'd be able to recreate any of the things Jen had done to make her look different. She was terrible with makeup, felt uncomfortable in decent-fitting clothes and didn't know if she could jab the wig pins into her scalp with as much glee as Jen had done.

"People are starting to talk, Laurel. Murder is murder even without the feud. Add the Delaneys and Carsons, and my store is a veritable gossip station."

"People have too much time on their hands, then. The murder has nothing to do with the feud."

"Then why are you suddenly being seen all over the place with the Carsons?"

It was stupid to be caught off guard by that. Laurel knew how this town worked. The Delaneys didn't go into Rightful Claim, ever, let alone twice in one week. And loud, disruptive Carson motorcycles did not make their way up to the Delaney Ranch. She'd been so focused on the case and clearing Clint, she'd been sloppy with anticipating how the town would react.

Or maybe that's Grady's influence. Just the thought of Grady filled her with... Well, it was irritation, but something in addition to that annoyance Grady normally evoked. And she was all too afraid it was familiar. A tingle. A shutting down of her rational brain. That same stupid thing that used to sizzle through her when she'd been a teenager hanging out with his sister and would catch a glimpse of him.

"Laurel. What's going on? Really. I know you can't share all the police stuff, but you can share the *you* stuff."

Her stuff? There was no *her* stuff. There was her job and her duty to this town and that was her entire life. She was proud of that. She *was.*

But something about Grady's obnoxious comment about chemistry had dug inside of her and stirred up all the lonely she so often ignored.

Like some sort of horrible cosmic sign, her phone vibrated with an incoming text message.

Jen snuck a quick glance at the sender's name, which read *GC*, and frowned.

"Yes, I'm going to ask who GC is, and yes, it better not be Grady Carson."

"Jen."

"I thought you grew out of this."

"Grew out of what?"

"Oh, like it wasn't obvious when we were in high school that you mooned over the guy?"

"Pot. Kettle," Laurel said, pointing to Jen and then to herself. "Ty Carson is back in town, by the way."

Jen's entire body stiffened. Yeah, Laurel might be stupid and a little bit weak in the head when it came to Grady, but her sister had no moral high ground to stand on. Laurel had only ever *looked.* She was pretty sure her sister had done more than that with Grady's cousin back in the day.

Ignoring her sister's waves of disapproval, Laurel brought the message up on her screen.

Gaskill here. On alert. Do. Not. Come. Here. Will report back.

"Well. Time to put my plan into motion," she said, taking one last glimpse at herself in the mirror. Anyone who knew her and looked right at her might figure out who she was, but if she stayed in the shadows, kept a low profile, she could sit next to Hank Gaskill and listen to everything he had to say.

Maybe it would be pointless, but maybe it wouldn't. She had to try. She'd sent Hart over to search Jason's place while she'd been at the mine, but he hadn't come up with anything. She'd take another look herself tomorrow, but for now she had to work on the people involved. The leads she *did* have.

"I should go with you."

"I believe the point of the disguise is, you know, Delaneys not going into Rightful Claim."

"Someone should go with you. I don't like you going there by yourself."

"It's police business, Jen. It's hardly dangerous. I'm just going to listen for some information that I may or may not even find. If someone is with me, it ruins the whole point."

"You're going to Grady's bar. That's not *all* police business."

"I don't know why you suddenly think I can't control myself, but I can. Besides, looking at Grady and Grady looking back are two very separate things." Which was probably not the way to convince her sister she didn't have a thing for Grady.

"You don't honestly think Grady Carson has never looked back at you."

Laurel turned her attention from her reflection in the mirror to her sister. After all, she and Jen looked a lot alike. Jen's hair was a shade lighter, and her eyes had hints of hazel. They were only about ten months apart, and they'd always been close.

But Jen had always been into the whole girlie thing. Understanding how to put on makeup and dressing to attract attention. Laurel had never been comfortable with that. She was more interested in police procedure and appearing tough and untouchable. She'd always wanted to be a cop, and a female cop *had* to be a little untouchable.

So, it didn't matter if her mind on occasion wandered to Grady, and touching him. It was all…fantasy. And irrelevant to her current situation at hand. "This conversation is ridiculous. I'm going to go do my job. Beginning and end of story."

"Fine. But I want regular text updates and I want to know when you're home. In fact, I'd feel even better if you come back here when you're done and assure me it was all police work and nothing dangerous."

Laurel stood and stepped out of the bathroom, adjusting the bra holster that wasn't comfortable, but the only way to conceal her gun effectively. At least in the jeans Jen had loaned her, because all of Jen's dresses were far, far, far too short for Laurel's taste.

"I'll text you when I get home."

"I don't like that you're wearing that gun. That means you think something bad is going to happen."

Laurel took a deep breath. "No, it means I'm on duty. You know who you sound like right now."

Jen wrinkled her nose. "Much as I hate sounding like Dad, it *is* a terrible feeling to know you're going off into danger."

"You're not usually this silly about my work stuff. What's going on?"

Jen crossed her arms over her chest. "Nothing is going on except you're not usually walking the line between Delaney and Carson while investigating a murder. A murder of someone we're related to, I might add."

"It's my job, Jen. I do it well." She picked

up the purse Jen had laid out for her to match the outfit. A little clutch that made no sense to Laurel. "What do you do with this thing? There's no strap. How am I supposed to attach it to myself?"

Jen rolled her eyes. "You carry it. It's cute. Not everything has to be functional."

"In my world it does." But she was playing a part. A part her sister had helped her get ready for. She turned to Jen and pulled her into a hug. "Thank you for helping me. You know I appreciate it."

"You owe me. Stay away from Grady Carson. Please just listen to me on that. Even if you take out all the feud nonsense, the Carsons are not meant for us. Period. I don't want you getting hurt by that moron."

"You ever going to tell me what happened between you and Ty?"

"Nothing happened between me and Ty. Ty Carson does not exist as far as I'm concerned. You should go. Policewoman business awaits."

Laurel rolled her eyes. She'd always been close with her siblings, but none of them had ever poked much at each other's romantic lives. It was considered a separate, no-go zone. Laurel wasn't sure why things were that way, but she supposed it was small-town complications. Everyone else poked into everyone else's business enough, why add to it?

Besides, Jen's worry was irrational, and Laurel shouldn't keep defending herself. It was pointless. She was not going to get *involved* with Grady Carson. No matter how much chemistry they had or how much he wanted her to admit it.

She had bigger things to worry about than chemistry. Carsons. Delaneys. Bent and feuds. She had a murder to solve.

And solve it she would.

GRADY WAS LOATH to admit that running a bar and trying to eavesdrop on someone was at cross-purposes. Any time he got remotely close to Hank's table and was able to overhear something of the conversation, someone called his name or clapped him on the back and asked him a question. Men made loud, raucous jokes in his direction and women offered smiles and innuendo and whatever.

It was something he usually enjoyed, the banter and flirting. The noise, the conversations. But today it only served to piss him off.

If he couldn't get any of the information

Laurel needed, he'd have to admit he failed. That galled for too many reasons to count.

He was not a guy who had to prove himself to people. He was what he was, and anyone who didn't like it could go to hell. The only person who had ever challenged that had been his dear old deadbeat dad.

And Laurel Delaney.

If he didn't get the information she needed, *she* would, and it seemed like adding insult to injury to fail at this, as well as know that she inevitably wouldn't.

The saloon doors swung open and Grady glanced up at the latest patron as he always did. There were a few people who tried to stir up fights in his bar, and he liked to cut them off at the pass.

But this customer was a woman. She looked vaguely familiar, but he couldn't quite place her. Dark eyes scanned the bar, moving past him rather quickly.

He frowned. She wasn't a regular or a known troublemaker, or he would have been able to place her. She didn't look like any Bent resident he knew. Something prickled through him, though, some kind of omen, as if he *should* be paying attention.

He shook his head. He was being some kind of paranoid, hyperalert idiot because he'd let Laurel's crap get into his head, and that just wasn't acceptable.

He focused back in on his target. If he could go clean off the table next to Hank, he might be able to hear *something* before someone bothered him again.

But just as he pulled the rag out of his back pocket, the woman who'd just entered slid into a chair at the table he'd been about to pretend to clean.

"It's not clean," he said gruffly.

"I don't mind," she replied airily.

Something about that voice… Grady glanced over at her but she studiously ignored his gaze. What was going on here? He thought about asking her if he knew her, but he was a little afraid she was some unhappy ex-lover. He didn't have time for that, and she didn't seem interested in rehashing anything.

"Get you something to drink?"

"A Coke, please," she said, her head turned so far away from him he could only see curly blond waves of hair and the peekaboo of an ear.

"Be right back."

She nodded, tucking her hair behind her ear. Which was when he saw it. The little wink of a silver star earring. Which Grady supposed could be a coincidence. Maybe tiny silver star earrings were all the rage and young women everywhere were wearing them.

But the woman's behavior, her voice, those familiar eyes darting all over his bar… He reached out and grabbed her wrist. When she jerked her gaze toward him, all flashes of gold fury, he very nearly dropped his jaw.

"What do you think you're doing?" he demanded. He was more than a little angry she'd fooled him for as long as she had with that ridiculous blond wig and clothes that actually fit her all-too-enticing body.

"Nothing," she hissed. "Now, if you would get me my Coke."

He gave her hand a tug. "Come over to the bar so I can get a tab started for you."

She held firm in her seat, staring him down with those dark, expressive eyes. "That won't be necessary," she said, over-enunciating each word.

She nodded her head toward Hank's table as if to tell Grady to stop in case someone in the group might overhear. Maybe he should. But he'd told her not to come in here. He'd told her he could handle it.

But he *wasn't* handling it. Even if her disguise didn't do much, if she sat here and sipped a Coke she had a far better chance of hearing something than he did. No one would recognize her if she calmly sat there. No one would believe Laurel Delaney was in Rightful Claim in a blond wig with an actual hint of cleavage showing.

Damn it.

He released her wrist. "One Coke coming right up," he muttered. Because he was *not* his father, and could back off even when he was irrationally pissed.

"Who's that chick?" Ty asked as Grady moved behind the bar and grabbed a glass.

Grady was an excellent liar in most situations, but he always hesitated at lying to family—especially Ty, Noah and Vanessa.

But this was important and bigger than him. "Some out-of-towner. She said she came in looking for a little Wild West charm."

"Is that a euphemism?" Ty asked with a grin.

Grady filled the glass with Coke and tried not to scowl. "Guess we'll find out," he muttered and headed back for Laurel and her stupid disguise.

Everything about the situation grated. The fact his hands were tied. The fact she was the one sitting there in a blond wig. So, he did what he always did when she irritated him.

"You make a hot blonde."

She glared at him. "Did you know that at a restaurant or bar, you don't have to tip the proprietor?"

"Says who?"

"The law," she returned, giving him a haughty look before glancing over at Hank's table.

He should let her be. Let her eavesdrop. Let her do her *job*, but he slid into the seat opposite her instead. When she didn't object or even send him a nasty glare, he decided he'd do her a favor in return by not asking her how she came upon a wig and clothes that actually fit.

She grabbed the sparkly purse that looked about as much like Laurel as the curly blond hair. Everything about her right now was the opposite of Laurel, and it was a little annoying to find he rather preferred her to be *her*.

She scribbled something on a piece of paper

and casually slid it over the surface of the table toward him.

He flipped over the paper and read the question in her neatly printed letters. *Who are the others at the table?*

He wanted to make a quip about her needing his help, and he doubted the table of three men next to them would notice, but he could be subtle. He wrote down the names of the men Hank was sitting with and returned the paper to her.

She read the names quickly, then slipped the paper into her sparkly handbag. She daintily sipped her Coke and studiously ignored him.

"Most female strangers who come into my bar flirt with me." He flashed a grin.

She rolled her eyes so far back in her head it must've hurt.

"Of course, you don't strike me as the type of person who knows how to flirt."

She curled her lip at him, as he'd hoped, but she didn't snipe back. Merely straightened in her chair.

Grady couldn't help the fact his gaze drifted to the hint of cleavage, and the whole outfit, really. Laurel Delaney actually had a body under there, and he couldn't even be surprised because the baggy clothes and fierce appearance no doubt served her in her job. And, unfortunately for her, in a small town you didn't get to be someone else once you clocked out of your job. Laurel Delaney *always* had to be Deputy Delaney, or risk a lot of things.

Why did he have to *understand* this infernal woman?

The table next to them laughed uproariously, but as Grady glanced over just like Laurel did, he imagined she saw the same thing.

The two men at the table with Hank were laughing, but Hank wasn't. He was staring down the bottom of his drink. Abruptly, he pushed out of his chair. "Going to grab a smoke," he grumbled to his jovial companions.

Hank wasn't even three steps toward the door before Laurel was picking up her purse. Luckily Grady was paying enough attention he could grab her hand before she got up. "Don't you think about it."

She glared at his hand on hers. "Don't *you* even think about telling me what to do."

"What do you think you're going to do after you follow him?" He leaned forward so that no one could hear them, though no one was paying any attention. "Ask for a cigarette? Smoke one? You?"

She jerked her hand out of his grasp. "If that's what it takes. Don't follow me or I will be forced to arrest you for getting in the way of a criminal investigation."

"I don't think that's legal, princess."

"I don't think I care. Stay here."

He could've grabbed her again. He could do a lot of things. But the fact he needed to get through his thick skull was that Laurel was a *cop.* She was investigating an actual murder case, and he didn't have any claim to sit here and tell her what to do.

If she wanted to be stupid and go have a smoke with Hank, as if that would get her any information, well, that was her prerogative.

She stood and walked out the same way Hank had. Grady scowled as he watched her go, her hips swaying mesmerizingly in the tight denim.

Which was *really* unfair, all things considered.

He'd give her ten minutes. Tops. And then he was going after her.

Chapter Seven

Laurel pushed through the swinging door and walked out of Rightful Claim with her heart beating a little too hard in her chest.

It had rattled her that Grady had seen through her disguise so quickly. But she'd grown up with Grady. She'd only met Hank Gaskill once in passing. Granted, it had been this morning, but why would he expect the blonde in a bar to be the brunette in Jason's office he'd talked to for five seconds?

She inhaled and exhaled, slowly walking toward where he leaned against the corner of the building, lighting a cigarette. He took a long drag and Laurel steeled herself to approach him.

"I don't suppose I could borrow a cigarette?" she asked, making her voice a little breathless and then berating herself for it. Over-the-top was suspicious.

"How can you borrow a cigarette? Plan on giving it back once you smoked it?"

Laurel couldn't tell if his response was snarky or flirty. That was always the trouble. While she could read murderous intentions or abusive husbands or drug addicts, she really wasn't very good at reading the opposite sex's reaction to her. There were always too many mixed messages and ulterior motives and it just didn't make any sense.

But she was on a job, playing a part. She wasn't Laurel Delaney. She was someone else entirely. So, she smiled as sweetly as she knew how. "Truth be told, I'd just like a puff of one. I quit a few years ago and I have just had the worst day."

"Well, this is the bad day corner," Hank replied and held his lit cigarette toward her.

Luckily, Laurel had seen enough bad movies to know you didn't take a deep inhale of a cigarette when she'd never smoked a day in her life. She put her mouth to the cigarette for a second and then pulled it away, pretending to sigh heavily as if it was a great relief.

"Thanks," she offered, offering the cigarette back to Hank.

He shook his head, tapping another cigarette out of the package he held. "Keep it. Had a rough day myself."

Laurel smiled understandingly. "They must really be going around, huh?"

"Yeah." His gaze moved down her body and back up, a kind of subtle checkout she probably wouldn't have caught if she wasn't looking for clues for a murder case.

"What's your sob story?" he asked.

"Just your average 'lost my job, boyfriend kicked me out' type thing. You?" she asked, sounding awfully casual if she did say so herself.

He shrugged and stared off into the dark, taking a deep drag of his cigarette before he replied. "Friend died."

"That's awful. Was he sick?"

Hank shook his head, and no matter how badly Laurel wanted to press, she knew that would only look weird coming from a stranger.

He looked her up and down again. "Why'd your boyfriend kick you out?"

"Oh." Laurel worked up her best sheepish smile. She was playing a very strange game here, but if it got her *any* information, did it matter? The important thing was if Hank thought she was available and interested he might tell her more about what he knew of his dead friend.

She had no other leads and a town whispering about murder and Delaneys and Carsons, so, sometimes the end justified the means.

"I may have kissed another guy," she said quietly, conspiratorially. "We'd been together a few years, and it just got boring, you know?"

Hank's mouth curved a little bit. "Wouldn't know. I must get bored before a few weeks is up."

Laurel laughed right along with him.

"You want to go back inside? I'll buy you a drink."

"Your friend died. I feel like *I* should buy *you* a drink."

Hank smiled. "Okay. I'll let you."

Grady wouldn't like that, Laurel knew. He'd think she was being stupid or something. But she couldn't care what Grady would like. She couldn't care what kind of lines she was tiptoeing on either side of right now.

If she had a drink with Hank, he might say *something* that could be a lead. Sometimes strangers were the best people to confide in. It wasn't as though he was the murderer. This morning he clearly hadn't known Jason was dead. But that didn't mean he might not know how or why.

Hank finished off his cigarette and flicked it into the street. Trying to hide how little she'd smoked, Laurel slipped hers into the ashtray canister on top of a trash can.

"Hank," he offered, holding out his hand to shake.

Laurel smiled and ordered herself not to panic at how many lies she was weaving. "Sarah," she offered, shaking his hand in return.

"You're not from Bent."

"No. Fremont. Well, that's where I lived with my boyfriend, but now I need a place to crash. So, I came to Bent to stay with my cousin for a bit."

"Oh, yeah? Maybe I know her. What's her name?"

Laurel fiddled with her clutch, trying to look like she was doing something purposeful while she tried to come up with the best lie. "Dylan Delaney." She figured using her brother's name was better than using that of any of her female relatives. And she couldn't use a Carson name. God knew they'd never back her up.

"Don't you know the Delaneys aren't supposed to be in Carson bars?" Hank asked with a grin.

Laurel smiled as flirtatiously as she could possibly manage. "I've never been very good at doing what I'm supposed to do." What a laugh.

"Well, then let's head inside and let you buy me a drink."

Laurel nodded and tucked a strand of hair behind her ear and turned toward the door.

Which burst open—and hit her square in the face.

GRADY SLAMMED HIS palms against the outward-swinging door, but instead of a satisfying, loud swing there was only a thump followed by a squeak.

It was not possible that he'd…

Gingerly, he pushed the out door again, this time meeting with no resistance, but when he stepped onto the well-lit boardwalk in front of his saloon, blonde Laurel was standing there holding her nose.

Again. For the second time in as many days.

Dark eyes met his, flashing all-too-enticing gold fury. "What is wrong with you?" she demanded.

"Me? I wasn't the one standing on the other side of the *out* door, sweetheart. That's why we have big signs that say *Out* and *In*, so people don't get knocked into unless they're drunk or stupid." No matter how acidic his voice was, his chest pinched painfully. Which was beyond stupid. She'd been the idiot standing on the wrong side of the wrong door.

Hank handed Laurel a bandanna from his back pocket, which she put to her bleeding nose.

"I think you owe her a drink on the house, man," Hank said, a little too cheerfully.

Grady raised one eyebrow at Hank and didn't move another inch of his body. Just stared down the little prick. "You think so?"

Hank wilted and looked away. Coward.

"Come with me and we'll get you cleaned up," Grady ordered Laurel.

"No, thank you," she replied, biting off each word.

"You should let him clean you up, Sarah. Get some ice and we'll get our free drinks. Okay?"

Hank patted Laurel on the shoulder, seeming a little too jovial for the situation.

"Shall we… *Sarah*?" Grady offered, gesturing at the door. Specifically the *In* side of the door.

She tried to smile. He could tell she really, really tried. And if she didn't have a handkerchief pressed to her nose, he might have found it all funny. As it was, he took her arm far too gently for his own liking and pulled her inside and through the loud, crowded bar.

He motioned Hank toward Ty. "Ty, get this man two drinks on the house." Ty nodded and Hank walked up to the bar while Grady propelled Laurel toward the back. When he started leading her toward the stairs up to his apartment, she jerked out of his grasp.

"I'm not going to that stupid apartment of yours and you are not ruining this for me." She pulled the handkerchief away from her nose. He didn't think it was quite as bad as the last one, but there was a slight smudge of blood underneath.

She looked at the bandanna and shook her head. "How. How is it possible? Twice in one week you smash me in the nose."

"Might I remind you that in the first instance, *you* ran into me. And in the second instance, I was going out the *out* side of the swinging doors. That's why they have the signs on them. You don't stand next to the out one, because people push *out* of them."

She closed her eyes, standing still as she breathed in, and then out. In and then out. Clearly trying to calm herself. When she reopened her eyes, all of that fury had been smoothed out of her features. "Grady, why were you coming out at all?"

"Guess I just wanted to witness how far you were willing to go for a little information. Call it curiosity."

"You are…" She shook her head. "I cannot work with you. I don't know why I ever thought that would actually be beneficial. Stay out of my way. Stay out of this case."

"You can't be serious."

"I can't include you in this if this is how you're going to act. I need you to listen to me. I need to trust that I can do something without you swaggering in and breaking my nose."

"It isn't broken." And he was behaving like a…like a contentious, surly teenager. "Stay here," he grumbled before stalking back to the kitchen. He grabbed one of the ice packs they kept in the freezer for bar fight injuries.

When he returned, he held it out to her. She took it, and placed it on the bridge of her nose with a wince.

He hated what he knew had to come next. Hated it beyond measure, but he hadn't gotten through life without having to do a few things he hated. He had a strict moral code for himself, no matter how a Delaney might sneer her nose at it. It didn't allow acting like a punk.

"I'm sorry."

She blinked at him, and he wanted to rip that idiotic wig off her. "What did you say?"

"I said, I'm sorry," he repeated, shoving his hands into his pockets. He wasn't going to *explain* that he'd charged out of the saloon and pushed that door far harder than he'd needed to, but he would apologize for causing some harm.

"For what part?"

"The nose part."

"Is that all you're apologizing for?" she asked coolly.

"You're right that's all. We're in this together, and I wasn't about to let you get dragged off in the dark by some—"

"We aren't in this together. This is not an equal partners thing. I am the detective. You're an informant at best. I need you to act like one instead of the over-the-top, makes-trouble Starsky to my Hutch."

"I'm sorry… Did you just make a Starsky and Hutch reference? What thirty-year-old makes a Starsky and Hutch reference?"

She all but growled in frustration. "I'm going back to Hank. You are not going to interrupt me. You are not… Is it me?" she demanded.

"Is what you?"

"That people think I can't hack it at my job. All of a sudden I have a *real* case and people are worried about me and think I can't handle myself. That I need help or protection or whatever. So, based on you and my sister's actions today I'm wondering, is it me? What kind of vibe am I putting off that makes you think I am incapable of handling myself?"

She flung her arms up in the air, clearly exasperated and pissed and maybe even a little hurt, and why could he *see* all that in the set of her mouth and the lines in her forehead? As if he knew what she was feeling just by looking at her. As if he'd spent a lifetime memorizing every emotion that flitted across her face.

Bull.

"Speaking from your sister's standpoint, she cares about you. I think if she were in some sort of dangerous situation, no matter how well-equipped she might be, you would worry about her, too. And express that worry. I believe that's called family love and devotion."

"Okay. Fine. Maybe you're even right. What's your excuse? Don't you think a woman can hack it?"

"Vanessa is my sister. Believe me, I know what women can hack."

"Then what? Why is it that you can't stand down and let me do my job? I'm a Delaney? You think I'm soft? You—"

"Maybe I don't like watching you smile and flirt with a stranger." Which shut her up. And was the only reason he said it. Not because it was true.

Her eyebrows drew together and he didn't know how a woman who was clearly intelligent and yes, fantastic at her job, could be so completely dense.

"Why would that bother you?" she asked as if there was no reasonable answer.

"Maybe, on occasion, I'd like it if you smiled at me." Which in fairness to Laurel wasn't a *reasonable* answer.

"That doesn't make any sense," she persisted.

"Why not?" he demanded, leaning closer. Closer and closer, making her eyes widen and the air between them crackle with electricity. It was an electricity he'd avoided his entire adult life out of duty, out of a healthy belief in the history of Carsons and Delaneys and Bent and destruction.

But Laurel stood there staring at him, her eyes a shade of dark, unfathomable brown, and no matter that she had that wig on, and makeup making her lips redder and her eyes smokier, she was so wholly *Laurel.*

"You're a Carson," she said on a whisper.

He stared at her for something like a full minute, and then he laughed. Because Ms. Doesn't Believe In The Feud thought he couldn't want her to smile at him. All because of his last name and hers.

He supposed he had two choices here in this little back room, empty since everyone working was up front at the bar. He could let her go back to Hank, find out whatever information she'd hoped to find, and wash his hands of messing with her or her investigation.

Or, he could do what he should have done fifteen years ago when he'd caught Laurel Delaney snooping around his room after a sleepover with his sister.

She dropped the ice pack from her nose, clearly still confused, and clearly ready to get back to cop mode.

"Grady, I—"

But he couldn't stand it. He cupped his hand around her neck and pulled her mouth to his.

Chapter Eight

Grady Carson was kissing her.

On the mouth.

She was sure there was something she was supposed to do about that, but her brain was all crackling static while her body…took it. She absorbed the feel of those full lips on hers, the warmth of his rough hand on the back of her neck, holding her still and there as his mouth took hers like they'd been doing this for centuries. Like everything about this kiss was right exactly as it should be.

She knew, somewhere, that was all wrong, and yet sensation seemed to mute that knowledge. Sweep it away into some strange, distant part of her. So distant it didn't seem weird to lean against him, to open her mouth to him, to press her palm against the hard, hot wall of his chest.

When he broke the kiss, slowly, so slowly, easing her body away from his, she had to tell herself to breathe, to open her eyes, to *think*. But all she saw was the vibrant blue of Grady's gaze, and the only thoughts she could manage were in gibberish.

She tried to inhale but it was shaky, the exhale unsteady. Everything felt jittery and unstable, and somehow she was still leaning toward Grady, only his arms keeping her upright.

She shook her head, trying to find sense or reason or some grasp of what was happening. She managed to rock back on her heels, holding herself upright so Grady's arms fell away.

He didn't say anything. He didn't move. If it weren't for that intense, heady gaze of his, she might have thought he was wholly unaffected. She wasn't sure he was *affected*, but he wasn't exactly…

Well, she didn't know. *He'd* kissed *her*. She didn't know why. She didn't know why she'd kissed him back. She didn't *know*, and that was her least favorite feeling in the world.

"I… I don't know what that was." She wasn't even sure she knew her name.

Laurel Delaney. Delaney. Deputy Laurel

Delaney, and if you recall, you have a murder to solve, not a Carson to kiss.

Kiss. Grady had kissed her. Kissed her with his mouth. His tongue. She could only stare at him because surely, surely no matter how… *wow*…that kiss was, he'd lost his mind.

His mouth curved in that infuriating way, except now she knew what that felt like against *her* mouth and she couldn't muster irritation because she was just…jelly. Boneless, spineless, thoughtless jelly.

"In my world they call it a kiss."

In her world it was something far more primitive than a kiss. Kisses were nice. Affectionate. Not a wild, all-encompassing thing.

"Go on back to your informant, smile some information out of him, and then…" He tilted his head, studying her with something in his expression she couldn't read. It was like humor, but not mean. He wasn't making fun of her, like she might have expected, but she certainly didn't know what he felt, or what he saw when he looked at her.

"Then what?" she asked, feeling entranced no matter how much she told herself to come back to reality.

"We can finish this discussion."

"I thought it was a kiss."

"Oh, princess. It was both."

Before she could make any sense out of *that*, he turned and walked away, disappearing into the main room of the bar while she stood in this little back area by herself.

By herself. Which was good. She could jam her brain back into gear by herself. She could think and plan and somehow compartmentalize, because she was here not to get even more confused about Grady. She was here to get information from Hank.

Hank, who was out there drinking a free drink and waiting for her. Hank, who certainly hadn't killed Jason, but might know *something*. Or have some clue whether he knew it or not.

Her job was her life. Had been since she'd joined the police academy. When she'd made time for any kind of…man-woman thing, it had been a relationship. Not a surprise kiss in the back of a bar from a man she wasn't even sure she *liked*.

It was all so complicated and confusing, and the point of being a cop was that it wasn't those things. There was right and wrong, legal and illegal, and the blurring of lines was only ever to find justice or the truth.

Which was what she needed to focus on. Grady had left, was clearly just messing with her or something. Which might make sense if he'd laughed or teased her for kissing him back, but he'd only told her to do her job and come back later to talk.

Talk.

Did he really mean talk?

She could not be worried about that. She placed the ice pack to the bridge of her nose, willing the icy jolt to get her to focus. On Hank, murder and her job. With a stern nod to herself, she walked back into the noisy, crowded bar, repeating four very important words over and over in her head.

Don't look at Grady. Don't look at Grady.

She focused on Hank, who was now sitting on a barstool, two empty glasses in front of him as he watched the TV above the bar intently.

Laurel approached, keeping her gaze steady on Hank and Hank alone. There was a phone placed on the seat next to him.

Laurel swallowed and picked it up. "Saving this seat for me?" she asked in her best throaty tone.

Hank glanced over at her and smiled.

"'Course. You're my free drink ticket." He winked as if it was a joke, but Laurel had to admit she wasn't so sure it was.

Which was fine. Drinking a little too much might convince Hank to tell her what he might know. Something Jason was into. Someone who was bothering him.

She placed his phone on the bar and slid into the seat. Hank waved at Ty down at the other end of the bar, and Ty made no bones about ignoring him.

Hank spared her a glance. "Don't worry. He owes you a drink. I'll get you one."

"No, it's—"

But Hank was already off his chair, striding down the bar to where Ty was serving.

Hank's phone vibrated and Laurel glanced at the screen. A text window popped up, and since Hank was occupied trying to scam himself into another free drink, Laurel nudged the phone so she could read the text.

There was no sender's name, only a number. The message read, Eagle Creek Park. 7. Bring folder.

Laurel frowned. Eagle Creek Park was an isolated state park that barely functioned as a park anymore. She didn't even think they had full-time staff. It was an odd place to meet anyone, unless you were teenagers hoping to get drunk or high. Which certainly didn't require any folders.

Hank returned, grumbling. "Said I had to wait my turn." He slid back into the seat, his hand going over his phone. "Maybe you should try..." He trailed off as he read his text.

"Everything okay?" Laurel asked.

Hank scratched a hand through his hair, then took one of the empty glasses and brought it to his mouth, trying to shake the last drops onto his tongue. His hand shook.

"What's wrong?" she asked, hoping it sounded like worry and compassion and not a cop demand.

"Nothing. Just gotta run. Hey, give me your number so I can hit you up sometime."

"Oh, sure, you want me to type it in?" she asked innocently, holding out her hand.

"Nah, just tell it to me." He sat, fingers poised on his phone screen, but Laurel didn't miss the way his eyes darted around the room.

It was almost ten o'clock, so he couldn't be rushing to meet the guy. Unless seven meant something else besides time. But what else could it mean? Eagle Creek Park was the location, and its address wasn't seven.

She rattled off a fake number. Much as she'd like to use this particular fake flirting to her advantage, she didn't want to push it too far. Especially when she might have to interrogate him as herself.

"Hope I see you around."

"Hope so," she offered cheerfully even though she wanted to stomp her feet and demand he tell her the answers. Instead she let him walk away.

But she had *something* to go on. Eagle Creek Park. Either seven tomorrow morning or seven tomorrow night. She'd be there both times and get to the bottom of this one way or another.

GRADY WATCHED HANK slink out of the bar. Based on the frustrated expression on Laurel's face, she hadn't gotten what she'd wanted out of him.

Grady shouldn't be happy about that. But, regardless, he had a few questions of his own. He slipped out the back, grabbing a half-full bag of trash as a prop, and pushed out into the parking lot. The Dumpster was right there, and he made a big show out of tossing the bag into the bin.

Hank approached a beat-up old truck and Grady cleared his throat. "Hey, Gaskill, right?"

Hank looked over at him suspiciously, so Grady did his best not to look intimidating. He probably failed in the dim light of a bar parking lot, a big man with a gruff voice.

"Fred Gaskill your kid brother?" Grady asked when Hank didn't respond.

"Yeah. What of it?"

"Clint Danvers. *My* kid brother. Who didn't get mixed up in trouble until good old Freddy came along." Which was a bald-faced lie, but might lead him somewhere at least. There were too many connections going on here, connections that led to his dumb brother.

Hank scoffed. "First of all, bull. Second of all, it ain't Freddy, and it ain't Clint, it's that chick that's got 'em wrapped around her pinky finger."

Which was certainly news to Grady. "Which one?"

"Lizzie Adams. She's got four kids in Fred's class following her around town, doing her bidding like she's some kind of TV mob boss. Those idiots are hard up enough to think she's going to put out if they do what she wants. Whatever trouble Clint's got, I guarantee you it started with her."

Lizzie Adams. Grady committed that name to memory. "Well, thanks for the tip, man."

Hank shrugged. "I've been telling Fred to stay out of her orbit for weeks, but he's seventeen. Imagine Clint is the same."

"More than," Grady grumbled.

Hank got in his truck and Grady offered a wave before heading back inside. Lizzie Adams. He didn't think a bunch of teenagers were really involved with murder, but something wasn't right.

He walked back into the bar, stopping at the sounds of crashing coming from the little kitchen. He peeked in to find Vanessa slamming things around with seemingly no purpose.

"Everything okay?"

She glared at him over her shoulder. "Fan-freaking-tastic. What's a Delaney doing in our bar? In a wig?"

"Don't worry about it."

Vanessa fisted her hands on her hips and glared at him, but he wasn't about to be intimidated by his little sister. "Hey, you used to invite her into our house. Consider this payback."

"I was a kid."

"And today I happen to be a grown man." He flashed her a grin that had her reaching for something to throw at him, so Grady picked up the pace and hightailed it into the main area of the bar.

Scanning the people sitting at the barstools, he was gratified to find Laurel still sitting there, typing things into her phone. Notes, no doubt. But she hadn't scurried off to do that. Her target had left, and she was still here. In his bar.

He wondered how long she'd stay. If she would share her information with him. If he should share his information with her. Or if all she wanted was to finish their discussion from earlier.

He grinned to himself, and as if that was some kind of beacon, Laurel glanced up and looked over at him.

She didn't grin back. She scowled. But when he nodded to the back room she slid off her stool and headed toward him. He didn't mind Laurel Delaney walking toward him at all, even in a blond wig.

"I need to talk to you. About the case."

His grin didn't falter. "That all?"

"Yes."

He made a considering noise to rile her up. "Upstairs is the only private place around here."

She rolled her eyes. "Fine."

He stepped through the opening into the back and headed for the stairs, but Vanessa stormed out of the kitchen.

"What are you doing?" Vanessa demanded. When Grady opened his mouth to tell her to mind her own business, she wagged a finger. "Not you." She moved the finger to point at Laurel. "You."

Laurel leveled her with a cool look, and didn't even pretend to be blonde Sarah. "Police business. That's all I care about, remember?" And with that she sailed past Grady and up the stairs.

Grady glanced at his sister with an eyebrows-raised questioning look, but Vanessa only huffed and stalked into the bar to start her shift.

Women.

He took the stairs, slowly, because he kind

of liked the idea of Laurel waiting for him. She was tapping her foot when he reached the top.

"Can we move this along? I have things to do."

"At your command, princess," he said, pulling his keys out of his pocket and unlocking the door to his apartment. He dramatically gestured her inside.

Once he closed the door, she didn't hesitate to start in on cop mode.

"I need some information out of Clint, and I don't think he's going to give it to me."

"I don't think he's going to give it to me, either."

"What about another family member? Vanessa, maybe?"

"Because she's known for her reason and charm? Pretty sure you were just on the brunt edge of that. What happened between you two?"

"A question only your sister can answer. I have no idea."

"Dad was pretty hard on her about being friends with you."

"Yeah, so was mine."

"He ever hit you?"

Laurel stilled, but she didn't wilt. "No. He

didn't." She blew out a breath. "I am not here to drudge up ancient history. Or Delaney-Carson nonsense. I saw a text Hank got that I can only assume is important or linked, and I need to know what Clint knows about Eagle Creek Park."

"You mean the place all the high school kids go to get high?"

"Yes. Exactly."

"I could probably get someone to ask him that without him bristling. Why do you need to know?"

"Because."

Grady crossed his arms over his chest and frowned down at her. "Try again."

"It's confidential."

"Fine, then I won't tell you what Hank told me out there in the parking lot."

"Hank didn't tell you anything."

Grady raised an eyebrow. "You calling me a liar? I believe back in the day that ended up with shoot-outs in the streets and a lot of Delaneys on the wrong side of a standoff."

"Tell me, and *then* I'll show you the text."

"Promise?"

She wrinkled her nose, clearly balking, but

eventually she pushed out a breath. “Fine, I promise.”

“Hank said his brother and Clint and a couple of the other idiot boys they hang out with are all gone over this girl, and she’s the cause of any trouble they get into. Girl named Lizzie Adams.”

“Adams? The man in charge of the mine is named Adams. These kids are connected somehow.”

“I agree.”

Laurel started moving toward the door, but Grady grabbed her arm. “Hey, you have to show me the text.”

“I have to go, Grady. I have to look into this. Make sure Lizzie Adams is—”

“You promised, princess,” he said, not letting her arm go no matter how she jerked it. “Now, spill.”

She grunted in frustration, but she pulled her phone out of her pocket with her free hand. “Let me go now.”

He did so, but stayed alert, because he wouldn’t put it past her to make a dash for it. And if she did, he’d have no compunction about throwing her over his shoulder. He’d enjoy it.

She held the phone out to him and he read the notes she'd typed.

"This is what his text said, verbatim. And this is the number."

"Eagle Creek Park. 7. Bring folder."

"So, I need to be at Eagle Creek Park at seven, and if he's not there in the morning, I'll go at night. But if Clint can get me some information—"

"What if it's not a time?"

"Huh?"

"What if seven isn't a time? It could be a… hike marker, a cabin—it could be a campsite. Hank wasn't just meandering out of here after a few drinks. If he didn't have somewhere to be, he'd be trying to get into your pants." Because it was damn weird Hank had hightailed it out of here.

"I have to go."

"Like hell."

"Grady, this is police bus—"

"Then call backup because I'll be damned if I'm letting you go to an isolated park all by yourself. I don't care if it's me or some cop crony of yours, but there's gonna be somebody."

"I don't have time for this. He's got a good

ten-minute head start on me, and Hank could be going into danger. Another isolated place like we found Jason? I'll call for backup on my way." She jerked the door open, but he followed.

"Fine, but I'm at your side until that backup shows up."

"Grady," she growled, already jogging down the stairs.

But he jogged right after her. "Sorry, princess, you don't have time to argue."

Chapter Nine

Laurel didn't have time to argue, and while she had half a mind to pull out her gun and use it on Grady to keep him put, she knew where night shift zones were, and she knew she could get to Eagle Creek Park long before any of the deputies on duty.

It *wasn't* smart to go alone, but it was hardly smart to go with a civilian. Especially this one.

But what choice did she have? She couldn't help thinking Hank was in danger, and she couldn't ignore that and wait for backup.

So, she got into her car, and let Grady get into the passenger seat no matter how much she shouldn't.

"Don't say or do *anything*," she instructed. She pulled her radio out from the glove compartment and switched it on. She relayed the information, what there was of it. A mysterious location in a big park, no idea of who was involved or if it was even criminal. It could be some romantic assignation. With folders.

She focused on the road, ignoring Grady's large presence in her passenger seat.

"You gonna take off the wig?"

She cursed under her breath and started digging for the pins keeping the wig in place. Every time she found one she plucked it out and tossed it over her shoulder. When Grady's fingertips skimmed her ear, she nearly jerked off the road.

"Easy," he murmured, far too close as she sped down the highway out of Bent. "Just going to help."

Somehow she focused on the road as Grady finished pulling all the pins out of her hair. Admittedly, her heart was beating too hard against her chest, but she could chalk that up to adrenaline and worry about Hank over the feel of Grady's fingers in her hair.

That man kissed you!

She could not even begin to think about that right now. Once it felt loose enough, she tugged off the wig and threw it in the back.

"Stick with brunette, princess."

"I'll keep it under advisement," she muttered,

flipping on her brights as they approached the park.

She squinted, surveying the side of the road. She knew the sign for the park had long ago been knocked over and not put back up, so the entrance was hard to find in the dark if you weren't looking for it. When she reached the entrance, she switched the lights back to normal. It would be hard to sneak up on anyone in a car, with the lights, the sound of an engine and the tires on the road, but she and Grady couldn't exactly hike the whole park, either.

"Do you know your way around?"

"I know the campsites are in the back. You take that left there," he said, tapping the windshield in the direction of a small gravel one-way street. "Campsites are numbered one through however many there are, if I'm remembering right. Road goes up, then around a cul-de-sac, so seven should be on our right as we drive up there."

Laurel nodded and navigated the turn onto the narrow road. She scanned the dark for the sign of a vehicle, a person, or anything that might lead them to believe someone was out here.

"How much space between campsites?"

Laurel asked as her headlights flashed against a crooked sign that read *Campgrounds closed.*

"Not much, so if we're only going to seven, we could stop here and walk. Can't imagine it taking more than ten minutes. We could surprise them. Well, assuming they haven't already heard the car."

Laurel nodded. It would be at least another twenty before backup could get to the park. She radioed out the plan to the officer en route, then brought the car to a stop in campsite one. She backed in, in case they needed to get out of here quick, before grabbing her flashlight and utility belt, and fishing the gun out of the bra holster.

She ignored Grady's raised eyebrows as he watched her, and got out of the car. She snapped everything into place except the flashlight, clicking it on as Grady quietly closed the passenger door and met her at the hood of the car.

"You should stay in the car," she said, knowing she was wasting her breath.

He huffed out a laugh. "Lead the way, Deputy."

She sighed heavily. "Stay behind me. Don't

make any noise. If you try to be a hero, I'll shoot you myself."

"Sure you will."

It was so incredibly annoying he knew her threats didn't hold any weight. But they didn't have time for bickering. She started walking up the gravel drive, training her flashlight on the ground and the signs alternatively, keeping her ears tuned to the sounds around them.

Wind whistled through the trees and against the grasses. Animals scurried through both. The dark took on a life of its own, a moving, unpredictable thing. Laurel kept her hand on her gun, and her flashlight at the ready.

As they reached the sign for campsite number five, she flicked off the light. Grady didn't say anything, and she gave them a few moments to adjust to the dark. It was a clear, cold night, but even the vibrant glow of the stars and moon above didn't make the dark any less daunting.

Laurel began to inch forward, keeping one foot on the gravel and one foot on the grass to make sure she was following the path of the road. When a hand grabbed her shoulder, she nearly screamed, but she bit it back in time, reminding herself *Grady* was behind her.

"Listen," he whispered into her ear. He was suddenly close enough she could feel his body heat, the slight movement of his breath against her hair, but she had more important things to focus on.

Listening.

It took a few moments, but finally she heard it. It sounded like the wind at first, but the more she listened, the more she picked up the cadence of speech in whispers.

She reached up and moved Grady's hand from her right shoulder to her left, then placed her own left hand over it. She patted it, trying to make a nonverbal sign for him to keep it there as they inched forward.

She needed to be close enough to hear what the whispers were, and she needed to know where Grady was. So, she stepped forward, and Grady followed, his tight, warm grip on her shoulder.

She pulled out her gun, wanting it at the ready in case whoever they came upon was armed as well. She hated that she wasn't wearing her vest, but she also hated Grady unprotected behind her and the fact Hank was in danger, no matter if he'd gotten himself in it.

The whispers got louder, but still Laurel

couldn't make out the words, and couldn't tell how close they were getting. With the open spaces and sparse clusters of trees, sound bounced everywhere.

Still she inched forward, forcing herself to breathe evenly, to focus on her mission. Keep Hank safe. Keep Grady safe. Then, find out what was going on.

There was a quick shout, and then the unmistakable sound of a gunshot.

Grady's hand clamped on her shoulder, but Laurel jerked out of his grasp and ran toward the shot.

WAS SHE CRAZY? Grady understood Laurel was a cop and all, but what woman went running toward a gunshot?

Then again, what unarmed, civilian man ran after a woman running after a gunshot? Apparently him. So maybe he had to question his own sanity.

When he caught up with her, she was crouching over a body. The flashlight was on a bloody spot on the guy's shirt.

Hank.

"Hank, can you hear me? Can you focus?"

Hank just groaned as Laurel pulled her cop

radio to her mouth, relaying the need for an ambulance ASAP, while her flashlight moved back and forth across the ground, clearly looking for clues as to where the shooter had gone.

She shoved the radio into its slot on her utility belt as she stood, then tossed Grady the flashlight and her phone. "Call 911 and have them walk you through keeping pressure on the wound."

"What are you going to do?" he demanded, and maybe he should have cared more about the fact Hank was moaning on the ground below him with a gunshot wound, but he was a little more concerned about Laurel ending up this way.

"I'm going to find the man who did this."

He opened his mouth to tell her something to the effect of *over his dead body* when sirens sounded in the distance.

"It won't be the ambulance, but it will be the cops. Call 911. Look after Hank. Let the police handle this."

And she meant *her*, which was against every impulse inside of him. Unfortunately, so was leaving a man bleeding profusely from a gunshot.

Laurel had taken off, already murmuring

into the radio that she needed the park secured. She'd left him the flashlight and it was all he could do not to grab it and rush after her. But Hank moaned, clearly trying to say something and unable to do so.

Grady cursed and used Laurel's phone to dial 911. How she had service out here he'd never begin to know, but as the 911 dispatcher answered, he explained his emergency and was given instructions on how to deal with the wound.

Hank groaned and thrashed as Grady applied pressure to the wad of fabric that had once been Hank's jacket. He placed the flashlight on the ground, beam pointed toward the wound, so he'd have both hands to work with.

"Didn't get it," Hank rasped, squinting at Grady as if he didn't see him. But he was talking, so he saw something.

"Didn't get what?"

Hank's hand thrashed around, his breathing becoming more labored even as Grady pressed on the wound. The ambulance needed to hurry.

"Pocket," Hank rasped, pointing to his left side.

Keeping the pressure as even as he could manage while also reaching across Hank's body, Grady grimaced and shoved his hand into the other man's pocket.

And pulled out a crumpled piece of paper.

"He didn't get it," Hank managed, his breathing getting shallower, his movements less erratic.

Grady frowned, trying to uncrumple the paper with one hand and read it in the beam of the flashlight. It was handwritten notes on a piece of graph paper. A list of dates, and next to each one a note. Most of it was nonsense to Grady. Names he didn't know, words he'd never seen before. But there was one line, dated two weeks ago, that was written in all caps.

CLEANUP WILL NOT MEET EPA STANDARDS.

Which meant nothing to Grady, and he doubted it would make sense to Laurel, either. But he figured out that whatever Hank, Jason and the man going around shooting people were involved in, it was centered at the mine.

It also meant whatever was going down at the mine was a big enough deal to kill, or try to kill, two men over. Blatantly. Without too much worry about being caught or repercussions if someone did put it all together.

And Laurel was out there in the dark.

If he hadn't been thinking about Laurel, about how many men she had out there with her now that the sirens had stopped and clearly the other cops were searching as well, he might have missed it.

A slight shuffle of leaves, the unmistakable sound of someone stepping on a twig or a branch or something. Then the eerie silence that followed.

Grady didn't move. No doubt if it were Laurel or any of the officers, they would announce themselves. Especially knowing they had a shooting victim.

It could be an animal, but animals typically didn't pause after they'd made a loud noise.

Grady didn't make any sudden movements. Whoever was out there had too good a vantage point, and hadn't shot yet. Which didn't mean he wouldn't, but it certainly meant he was considering not shooting him, too.

So, slowly, almost imperceptibly, Grady began to turn his head to look over his shoulder.

"Don't move," a faraway-sounding voice rasped.

"All right," Grady replied, keeping his head

exactly where it was, inflicting his tone with as much ease as he could manage.

"Who are you?" the man growled in an undistinguishable voice that didn't stay still. Grady couldn't tell if the man was pacing or just moving around.

"You think I'm going to tell a strange man in the woods who I am?" Laurel wouldn't approve of this particular method of dealing with a man and, presumably, a gun, but Grady had known his fair share of desperate men. He could handle this one.

He hoped.

The ambulance had to get here soon, and if it didn't, the officers would have to circle back. So, maybe at worst he ended up with a bullet to the gut like Hank and lived to tell the tale.

Worst-case scenario is probably bullet to the head, genius.

Grady pushed that thought away and focused on the task at hand. "Just trying to help a guy out here. I don't want any trouble."

The man made some scoffing sound and Grady tried to focus on his surroundings. Was there anything he could use as a weapon? Did Hank have anything on him that could be grabbed and used as a weapon before the guy shot him?

He just needed the thug to come closer so Grady could knock him down. He had no doubts he could win in a fair fight, no matter how big the guy was, but this man had a gun, and Grady had nothing.

"Step away from Hank."

Grady looked down at Hank's form illuminated by the flashlight beam. He'd gone still, but his breathing continued, labored as it was. Grady wasn't sure the man could survive if he lost any more blood.

And you're not going to survive with a bullet to the brain.

But he'd never been very good at backing down to bullies. "Why don't you just let my friend here—"

"What's in your hand?" the man demanded, and he'd either forgotten to use his raspy voice or just didn't care.

Grady looked at the paper. The last thing he wanted to do was give the evidence up, but if he could remember the date, and the exact verbiage of the all caps message, plus some of the names…

Suddenly the paper was torn from his grasp,

which gave Grady the chance he needed. He immediately kicked out, making contact with the man's shin. The man howled in pain, but unfortunately he didn't go down.

Which meant Grady had to take the pressure off Hank's wound. It would be precious time and probably precious amounts of blood, but they were both going to end up dead if Grady didn't fight.

So in a stealth move, Grady got his feet underneath him in a crouching position. As the attacker raised his arm, moonlight glinting off the gun in his hand, Grady lunged.

He rammed into the attacker, which sent them both sprawling, and Grady hoped the clattering sound mixed with crunching leaves was the gun falling out of his attacker's grasp.

Suddenly, over the sound of their grunts, Grady heard sirens, loud and clear. He looked up to see the flashing red, which was stupid, because it gave his attacker just enough time to land a blow that had his world going black.

Chapter Ten

Laurel swore and then swore again. She'd scoured the back of the park as much as she could manage with no artificial light, but there was no sign of the shooter. The only men she'd run into were the two officers she'd called in for backup.

"He could be anywhere. We just don't have the manpower for this kind of search," Deputy Clarion said disgustedly.

He was right, but that didn't ease Laurel's irritation or anger. Having someone *else* shot while you were investigating a murder wasn't exactly the thing stellar detective careers were made of. Especially when she had no suspects, no clues. Only forest and darkness and questions.

This was all her fault. She did everything in her power to push away the crushing sense of failure, but it rooted deep. She'd missed clues and hadn't thought things through, and another man was hurt because of her and could very well end up dying.

"We need to head back and make sure he hasn't doubled back," Laurel ordered, a little sharper than necessary, but she felt sharp and pissed.

She'd left Grady behind unarmed, and it was more than possible a man with a gun had outsmarted them, circled back, and was going to do his best to finish off the job of killing Hank. Because they were dealing with someone who was desperate enough to murder one man, and attempt to murder another. She didn't think he'd stop to consider the moral implications of murdering Grady as well.

She swore and increased her pace. "Keep your eyes peeled, but our focus right now is getting back to the victim," Laurel called over her shoulder, breaking into a jog. "If our suspect gets away, we're just going to have to chalk it up to a loss, but if our victim is finished off, or a civilian is, that's on us."

Her, really. She'd been the idiot to let Grady strong-arm her into bringing him here, and then she'd been the fool who'd left him to fend off anything that came his way with a dying man and no weapon. She'd left him defenseless.

The idea of Grady being defenseless was *almost* laughable. Grady was big and strong and inherently capable of handling himself, but he wasn't Superman. He couldn't fight off a bullet.

She heard the two other deputies huffing behind her so she walked faster. Through the trees and dangerous open areas, back to the campsites where she'd left Hank and Grady. Moonlight lit her way, and as she got closer, the flashing lights of the ambulance helped lead her exactly where she needed to be.

The fact the ambulance was there eased some of the worry clogging her chest. It had made it to the correct location, which meant Hank had a chance and Grady hadn't been hurt. Surely they'd gotten to Hank and Grady before anything had happened.

The suspect had probably made a run for it without a second thought to look back. He probably figured Hank was as good as dead and had gotten what he was after.

And yet somehow Laurel didn't feel any better. She got close enough to see Hank's body strapped to a stretcher and being lifted into the ambulance, but no Grady.

She swallowed down the panic. He was around here somewhere. Had to be. "Where's the other man?" she demanded of the paramedic as he closed the doors.

"What other man?"

"There was a man here guarding Hank, the victim."

The paramedic raised his eyebrows. "I didn't see anyone, and I've got to transport this man. He's lost far too much blood and is unresponsive."

"Wait. There was another man. There was another—"

"I have to go, Deputy, if you want this man to—"

They both stopped arguing when a loud groan came from somewhere nearby, along with the rustling of leaves.

Laurel immediately moved toward the sound and she was gratified the paramedic didn't take off.

"Grady?"

The response was a string of truly filthy curses.

"Give me your light," Laurel demanded of

the paramedic. He handed her a flashlight and she flicked it on, moving the beam of light up toward the groaning and cursing.

"Grady." He was sprawled out in a shallow gully. As she moved closer, he rolled onto his side, clearly tried to sit up and failed. "Don't move," she ordered, scurrying down the little swell of earth and kneeling at his side. "Oh, my God. Are you shot?"

"I don't know," he grumbled. "Am I?"

"Grady." She tried to run her fingers over his chest, but the paramedic was pushing her out of the way.

"Where does it hurt, sir?"

"Probably the bleeding wound in my head," Grady snapped back, and though he had some fire to his responses, even in the weird illumination provided by the ambulance lights and flashlights, Laurel knew he looked pale.

"Simon, we have to go," the other paramedic yelled from the ambulance. "This guy isn't going to hold on much longer."

"Got another one, Pete. Blunt force trauma to the head. Lost consciousness. Bring out the other stretcher."

Pete swore, but moved quickly and efficiently.

"I don't need a stretcher." Grady pushed

at the paramedic, and nothing made Laurel's blood run colder than the fact he didn't even budge the paramedic. Big, strong Grady Carson's push was ineffective at best.

She swallowed at the fear trying to lump itself in her throat. "Let them put you on the stretcher, Carson." She turned to the other officers she'd almost forgotten about. "You two, canvas the area. Anything you can find, you bag up. Got it?"

"Piece of paper," Grady mumbled as the two paramedics worked to move him.

"What?"

"Hank had a piece of paper. Something important. It's all a little fuzzy." He lifted a hand, but dropped it.

"A piece of paper. Okay, I'll look for one."

"What did that guy hit me with? I knocked his gun away."

He'd knocked the shooter's gun away, dear God. The paramedics started hefting him to the ambulance, and Laurel had to order herself to focus. Not on Grady, not on how badly he might be hurt, but on figuring out who did this.

"We're looking for a gun, something that could have been used as a blunt force trauma weapon and a piece of paper," she announced to the two deputies searching the area.

The ambulance revved its way out of the campsite parking space and Laurel had to force herself not to look at it. Grady was in good hands.

And hurt. Because of you.

She wasn't sure she'd ever been so close to crying on the job, but she ruthlessly blinked back the tears. "Anything you even question for a second, bag it. We need a clue."

She moved her beam to the gully Grady had been lying in. She didn't see anything outright, but it was covered in leaves. She reached into the part of her utility belt she kept rubber gloves in and pulled one on.

She began to sift through the leaves, looking for anything at all that wasn't natural debris. Anything that could have been used to hit Grady over the head.

She found the tiniest scrap of paper, white and dry, which meant it couldn't have been here long. She squinted at the words, but there weren't enough to make any sense out of it. Still, she placed it in her evidence bag.

Then her hand ran into something hard. She pulled it out of the pile of leaves and studied it. A shoe. A nice shoe at that. Men's. Big enough. With a sole hard and sharp enough to do some damage.

Laurel slipped that into the bag. She probably couldn't get an identity with a shoe, but it was certainly *something.*

"I found a gun," one of the deputies said a few yards south of her.

Laurel nodded. A scrap of paper, a shoe and a gun. It wasn't much.

But it was something.

GRADY HATED HOSPITALS. They were so white and every noise was so mechanical. He'd watched a few too many people die in hospital rooms. He'd been with all of his grandparents, holding hands or murmuring prayers, because his grandparents had raised him right in the shadow of everything else.

Then there was the time Dad had died. Grady trying to shield Vanessa, being pushed away as monitors went crazy and nurses jumped into action. And somehow feeling sad when all was said and done, even though his father had never been anything more than a mean SOB.

Grady blew out a breath and glared at the

door. They'd stitched him up and talked over his head about concussions and being watched overnight, and he was about ready to lose his usually impenetrable cool.

They were going to release him soon, or he was going to fight his way out. One way or the other. He just had to figure out whom to call. Noah or Vanessa or Ty. Hell, he should call Clint and demand some payment for what a mess he was in because of the kid.

But the only person he wanted to call was Laurel, and that was messed up.

When the door opened, Grady was ready to go after whatever poor soul dared darken his door without discharge papers.

"Mr. Carson," a young, timid thing asked, hovering there as though she were afraid of him. "There's a police officer here who wants to speak with you, and I couldn't find—"

"Is it a woman?"

"Um, well, yes."

"Send her in, then."

"Oh. Right. Well."

"Now," Grady growled, sending the girl scurrying out the door. A few seconds later, Laurel appeared. She was still wearing what she'd been wearing in his bar earlier, sans wig.

She'd tamed her hair back, though, in one of those serviceable braids she tended to favor. And she looked serviceable and a little bit formidable on top of it.

Hell, he wanted to get her into bed.

"Why are you torturing that poor candy striper or whatever it is she is?" Laurel asked, and he noted she hovered close to that door opening even as her gaze scanned his bandage.

"Because no one will let me out of this hellhole."

Her mouth flattened and she jammed her hands into her pockets. "Well, I need to take your statement."

"You came all this way to take my statement, princess?"

"Yes. Is your head a little clearer now, or should I wait until morning?"

"My head is just fine," Grady said, willing the snap out of his tone and failing. "Everything about me is just fine." To prove it, he slid off the hospital bed and into a standing position.

"Sit back down right this instant," Laurel demanded, crossing the room as if she was going to push him into bed herself.

"You ain't in charge of me, Deputy," Grady

returned, folding his arms across his chest and fighting back the dizziness that had taken over him. "The doctor is working on my discharge papers, so I can stand just fine." He glared down at her, but that scowl she'd been using seemed to fall away as she took in the bandage on his temple.

She looked…defeated. Sad. Guilty.

Hell.

"I just need to get your statement," she said quietly. "We don't need to argue."

"But arguing is what we do best."

Laurel shook her head faintly, and that weird cloak of sadness didn't leave her. "Did you get a look at the attacker?" she asked, pulling her ever-present notebook out of her pocket, along with a pen. "Any identifying marks or facial features that might distinguish them from other people? A height, weight or build."

It galled that he didn't have any answers, but he couldn't exactly make any up, so he had to be honest. "No. It was dark and I couldn't see anything except for the fact he had a gun. Did you guys find it?"

She swallowed and gave a sharp nod, her dark eyes soft and something else. Something he couldn't recognize no matter how many other emotions on her he could.

"Yes," she said, her voice rough. "We found it. Ideally it's traceable and this is over, but..."

"The murderers of the world don't usually use traceable guns."

"No, they do not. We also recovered a shoe, which was the weapon that..." Her eyes darted to his bandage again. "Did you have to get stitches?"

"Yeah. Ten. Must've been some shoe."

"It was sharp. Hard-soled." She inhaled shakily and he didn't understand what this was. Just guilt over someone hurting him? He wasn't sure he understood why she should feel that way. Which made it hard to know if he wanted to comfort her or tease her.

"I'm so sorry," she said, all earnestness and Laurel. Just Laurel, this bastion of right and fighting wrong.

Which answered that question for him. He didn't want to tease her when she was all soft. "For what?" he demanded a little bit too brusquely.

"I shouldn't have left you there. I shouldn't have taken you there at all, but I really shouldn't have left you with a hurt man completely unarmed. I should have known or predicted he'd double back and… He could've killed you, Grady. So easily. He could have killed you both, and I wouldn't have been able to do anything about it. And that… It was shoddy police work and I'm sorry that you got caught in the middle."

"See, I just thought it was one of those instances where you did your best but bad things happen because life is unpredictable," Grady returned gruffly, because he didn't want her guilt or her apologies. Not when he'd forced her hand, and not when… Well, she had done her best. He was no idiot.

"I should've known better," Laurel said firmly.

"How?"

"Because as a police officer you're trained to deal with these things. You are trained—"

"You're trained to know exactly where a murder suspect might go in the dark? In an isolated, enormous park that no one has been to in years and therefore has no brush cleaned up, no identifying markers, no nothing?"

"I am trying to give you an apology," she said through gritted teeth.

"I don't want your apology. I was the one

who made it impossible for you to go without me, and I'm sure glad I did. Because the fact I could stay with Hank made it certain *you* didn't both end up dead."

"It would've been in the line of duty. It would have been my job. It's not your job. You shouldn't have been there, and you shouldn't have gotten hurt, and it's my fault that you did."

"How long you going to self-flagellate, because I'm out until you're done."

Laurel threw her arms up in the air. "You are insufferable. And ridiculous. I'm trying to be nice and…and…be a good person, and you're throwing it back in my face!"

Even though his head was starting to throb, Grady couldn't help smiling. Maybe it was sick, but he sure liked seeing her irritated more than he liked seeing her…contrite or upset or whatever that was.

"I need your statement," she snapped, hitting her pen against the notebook, eyes flashing angry gold. "Tell me everything that happened once I left."

To placate her, he did just that. He went through calling 911, and trying to stop Hank's bleeding. He remembered the paper, but then things started to get a little gray. Not quite linear. There was something about a paper. Hank had a paper?

"You can't remember?" Laurel asked gently and he scowled at her.

"I remember. Some things. Bits and pieces, but I can't seem to put it all back together in the right order."

"I think that's a fairly common concussion symptom."

"It's not a serious concussion."

"But it is *a* concussion. And ten stitches."

"And not your fault. I probably would have gotten knocked around a lot worse if I hadn't been thinking about you." Which was not an admission he needed to make, except he was tired. Exhausted. His head hurt, and he didn't… He didn't want her guilt or her cop crap. He just wanted her.

"What do you mean you were thinking about me?"

"I was worried about where you had gone, and what might be happening to *you*, and I was listening for you. I heard a twig break and shuffling of leaves and then I knew someone was there. Which gave me time to prepare and fight back." But he couldn't remember much of the fight.

"You don't have to worry about me," she said, shoving her notebook and pen into her pocket. "I'm the cop."

"You're not invincible because of a badge," he snapped, wanting to shake some sense into her.

"No, but—"

"Just shut up," he bit out, because if she spent any more time talking about her line of duty, he was going to end up kissing her until they both forgot their last names.

Which was the number one thing he wanted, and not just because of this night. He couldn't remember a time he hadn't wanted a piece of Laurel Delaney, and the events of this night made him tired of pretending.

"I found a scrap of the paper you mentioned," Laurel said, using that cool cop tone that seriously tested his self-control. "It doesn't make any sense to me. But I took a picture of it." She took her phone out of her back pocket and handed it to him.

He looked down at the screen. It really was just a scrap. Two dates listed, then not even two full words after. He knew he'd looked at this. He'd looked at this paper and…

"It's okay if you don't remember," Laurel said gently. "It'll come to you. In the meantime, we have a shoe, a gun and the first real evidence-related lead we've had this whole investigation. And, unless either comes back as being Clint's, which I find very hard to believe, your brother is off the hook. Which means so are you."

Off the hook. Because Clint would be proven innocent. It didn't make him feel any better. In fact, it pissed him right off. "Like hell I am."

Chapter Eleven

Laurel didn't think Grady would ever make any sense to her. He should be relieved. He should be skipping out of the hospital room. Free.

But he was fuming. *Fuming.*

"Clint isn't a part of it," she repeated. Maybe the concussion was making it hard for him to think straight or understand everything properly. "Which means I don't need your help anymore. At least, there's no reason for you to help me. Your brother is in the clear. Probably."

"You really don't think I have a reason to still be involved in this?" Grady asked incredulously.

"Well—"

"Someone hit me over the head with a shoe and gave me a concussion. It could have been a lot worse, too. So, I am going to be a part of bringing him down."

"Grady," she began, doing her best to find a reasonable tone.

"Do not argue with me, princess. I am in this now. No one knocks me out and gets away with it. I've got a little revenge to enact."

"My job isn't about revenge. It's about justice, so you wanting revenge can't—"

"Consider my revenge justice. Now—"

A knock sounded at the door and an older woman in nurse's scrubs stepped in. "I have your discharge papers, Mr. Carson." She smiled pleasantly at Laurel. "And good, you have someone who can drive you home."

Laurel opened her mouth to argue. She should not be driving him home. He needed to call one of his cousins, or his sister or even Clint. Anyone who was not her.

She needed some distance from Grady. No matter if he had revenge *or* justice on the brain. She had let herself be compromised by all his irritating goading and charming smiles and that kiss, and she had done things she knew went against protocol.

Laurel *never* went against protocol.

But Grady flashed the nurse a charming

smile. “Yes, I got myself a ride home. Now let’s get me out of here.”

“We just have to go over some paperwork, I’ll need a signature, then you’ll be free.” Again the nurse turned to Laurel. “Will you be staying with Mr. Carson overnight?” she asked innocently.

Grady grinned. “Yeah, I think she owes me that.”

Again Laurel opened her mouth to protest, but there was no point in arguing in front of the nurse. There was no point in arguing, period. Grady would get her to do what he wanted. He always seemed to.

So, she would get him home to the Carson Ranch. The other Carsons would kick her out so fast her head would spin, and the fact that idea disappointed her was reason enough to go through it. She needed a Grady-ectomy and stat.

“Here is a list of symptoms you may have for the next few weeks,” the nurse said, handing Grady one of the sheets of papers she’d brought in. “You should avoid driving for at least twenty-four hours and tonight, if you’re sleeping, you should be woken up every two hours to make sure you’re responsive. All of these papers have information on how to deal with a concussion and when to call us, but mostly the main concern is if you're unresponsive or your symptoms get significantly worse." She went through the medications Grady could take and rattled off more instructions before letting him sign his release form.

"You are free to leave whenever you're ready," the nurse said cheerfully. "Take care of Mr. Carson," she added to Laurel before striding out of the room.

"Come on, driver. I'm ready to go home."

"I'm going to take you to the ranch and drop you off with your family," Laurel said firmly. No matter that looking at the bandage on his head made her want to touch his face. Press her cheek to his chest and listen to his heartbeat.

Maybe *she* had been hit over the head.

"You'll drive me to Rightful Claim and take good care of me all through the night," Grady returned, that sharp, wolfish smile on his face as he gathered his belongings.

What was wrong with her that she *wanted* that, and so much more? And, worst of all, she always kind of had, but she'd learned to keep her distance, to force her focus elsewhere. But

Grady Carson had always been that thing she couldn't want or have, and so she'd turned it off.

But it was impossible to turn off when he was *here* all the time, when he'd kissed her, when he was saying 'take good care of me all through the night' with that glint in his eye.

She wanted to be him for a second. To say outrageous things and not give a crap. She wanted to be *free* of all the rules and protocols she'd placed on herself. "I'm pretty sure she said no vigorous activity," she retorted.

Grady barked out a laugh and she hated the part of herself that was warmed by that. Encouraged. The part of her that wanted to fuss over him and, yes, have a little vigorous activity. It was a lot more than a concussion standing in her way of all that.

"That makes me wonder all kind of things about you, Laurel."

"I'll drive you to Rightful Claim, but I'm not your nurse. Someone from your family should come stay with you." Because she did not trust herself. A sad, pathetic fact.

"Someone from my family isn't the reason I have a concussion."

She knew he was trying to use her guilt against her. She knew she absolutely shouldn't let him. A good cop knew they weren't at fault for something that went wrong. It was the fault of the bad guys. Murderers and rapists and burglars—they were at fault when bad things happened.

But knowing something and feeling something were two very different things—hence her current predicament. She walked down the squeaky hospital corridor and toward the exit, warring with herself. With knowing and feeling.

She knew better than this and yet some part of her wanted to take care of Grady. She wanted to talk over the details of the case with him, and she wanted to be there when he remembered what he would inevitably remember. Something about that paper.

Grady slung his arm across her shoulder, casual as you please. "Don't think so hard, princess. You're giving me a headache."

"I think the concussion gave you a headache."

"Nah, it's you."

They stepped into the cold chill of late-night autumn. Or, more accurately, way-too-early morning. She led him to her car and felt a sudden wave of exhaustion roll over her. This had been the longest night and it felt as though nothing concrete or impactful had been accomplished.

You have evidence. You are making progress.

She was, but it was the knowing versus feeling thing again. She didn't *feel* progress. She couldn't seem to feel anything that wasn't futility, despair or frustration.

She glanced at Grady sitting in the passenger seat of her car. He had his eyes closed, and the white bandage stuck out against the tan skin and dark beard of his face.

It really wasn't fair he was so handsome, and that he was here, the living incarnation of her current life crisis. He was so many things she couldn't want, and yet did. Why couldn't her emotions ever follow the reason she was so desperate to live by?

"We going to sit here all night?" he asked, eyes still closed, voice a rumble in the quiet of the car.

"I'm not going to sleep with you," she said firmly, because if she put it out there, in real, spoken words maybe she could be sure.

"You've said that a few times now. I can only assume that means you think about sleeping with me an awful lot." He turned his head to face her, eyes open and far too blue, and he grinned.

But Laurel didn't have it in her to grin back. There was this out-of-control thing inside of her she didn't know how to rein back in, and she didn't know what to *do*—when knowing what to do was all she'd ever done.

"For the record," Grady drawled. "I don't think I have it in me tonight. But I never say never."

Laurel turned on the car and pulled out of the parking spot. "I didn't say never," she grumbled.

GRADY FELT NAUSEOUS and his head was pounding and if he had any energy at all, he would be tracking down the person who'd done this to him and bashing his head in.

He pulled his keys out of his pocket and unlocked the back doors of Rightful Claim, Laurel hovering behind him. Her presence was the only thing that kept him from actually punching something. Because somehow just her being there felt comforting.

He'd never thought to look for *comforting* in a person he spent time with before, but Laurel gave him all sorts of interest in the feeling. Especially considering his body felt like hell and working up any other interest probably wasn't happening.

Grady stepped inside and Laurel followed. He locked the door behind her and walked toward the stairs to his apartment. He paused at the bottom of them. Stairs he undoubtedly ran up and down a thousand times a day suddenly seemed daunting. Too much.

"They should've kept you overnight," Laurel observed in a brisk tone.

He scowled in her direction. "I'm fine."

"You're struggling," she said firmly.

"Then why don't you help me up the stairs and take good care of me?" he asked, trying to flash a cocky grin her way and failing mostly. All he could seem to do right now was grimace.

She rolled her eyes, but she stepped closer to him so that they were side by side. With a huff of irritated breath she cinched her arm around his waist.

"Come on. Let's go."

He looked down at her incredulously. She really thought she was going to help him up the stairs? "You're a slip of a thing."

She made a scoffing noise. “I only seem like a slip to you because you’re ginormous.”

“Ginormous, huh?”

He noted the faint blush that crept across her cheeks and wished he had the wherewithal to lean down and capture her mouth with his.

“I’m sturdy enough,” she continued, gauging the stairs in front of them. “Probably kick your ass in the PT test.”

“No. Definitely not.”

She began to take steps with him, and he didn’t lean on her so much as let her presence be a guide in keeping his dizziness at bay.

“We can test that theory sometime, but not today.”

Grady grumbled irritably and let her help him up the rest of the stairs. It was just that all of his limbs felt heavy. His body, his head, everything felt stonelike and sluggish.

“I cannot fully express the unfairness of being rendered this weak by a shoe.”

She patted his back sympathetically. “It was a very hard shoe.”

“Don’t placate me.” They reached his apartment door and he unlocked it before pushing it open and stepping inside. It was good to be back in his own place. In his own air.

"Go lie down."

"Yes, ma'am. I find your bossy so hot."

She muttered something under her breath and went over to his little kitchenette. She started looking through his cabinets, muttering all the while. Grady toed off his boots and sprawled out on the bed. The covers were all tangled at the end of the mattress and it seemed like far too much work to pull them up.

"Don't you have any tea?" Laurel asked, rummaging through his stuff.

"Yes, Laurel, I keep *tea* on hand. Do I seem like a *tea* guy to you?"

"Don't you have anything warm and comforting?"

He patted the bed next to him. "I have you."

He thought he saw her mouth curve a fraction and he'd mark that down as a success.

"You know you're impossible, right?" she asked, fisting her hands on her hips and doing her best to glare at him.

"You would not be the first person to tell me that. I believe that was the lullaby my mother used to sing me to sleep with."

"You should call Vanessa. She'd be in a much better position to take care of you."

"Vanessa? My sister Vanessa? She couldn't take care of a pet rock."

"Fine. Noah? Ty? They're your family." She had that soft, earnest look about her and he much preferred the almost smile he'd earned a few seconds ago.

"Right. Which means I don't get nearly as much enjoyment out of pissing them off."

"I'm not pissed off."

"No, you're guilty. Which pisses *me* off. Come sit next to me."

"I am not sitting on the bed with you."

"Can't control yourself around me, princess?"

"Grady."

"I want you to show me the picture again. I want you to go through everything that happened, and if you go through it, maybe it'll jog my fuzzy memory and I can put these pieces back together."

"I think you should sleep. I have to wake you up in two hours and see if you're responsive. Then we can go through all that."

"Then you're staying?" he asked.

"If you're not going to call anyone else, what choice do I have? I don't have any of their numbers. I could wrestle your phone from you, but

I have a feeling that wouldn't end up the way I'd like it to."

Grady chuckled. "No, baby, wrestling would not end the way you want it to."

"Get some sleep."

"I need to work through this or I'm never going to fall asleep." And he wasn't even just trying to get her into his bed. It was eating at him, all those murky pieces he couldn't remember.

She sighed heavily and shook her head as though she couldn't believe what she was about to do. Then she walked over to the bed. Gingerly and hesitantly she rested her butt on the very edge opposite him. She handed over her phone. "Here's the picture of the scrap we found."

"If I start scrolling through your pictures am I going to find something interesting?"

"In your dreams."

"Yes, interesting images of you have appeared in many of my dreams."

"Grady," she scolded exasperatedly.

"Okay. So we got there, and we heard the gunshot. We found Hank, and then you took off."

"First you argued with me, and then I took

off," Laurel corrected, sliding just a little bit more into the bed so she could stretch out her legs and rest her back against the headboard.

"Semantics," Grady replied. "I called 911. They told me to put pressure on the bullet wound. He was losing a lot of blood. I remember all that clearly." Grady looked down at his hands. For a moment he could almost see Hank's blood on them, but they'd washed that off at the hospital.

"How is Hank?" he asked, surprised at how rusty he sounded.

"He lost a lot of blood. He's still alive, but it's fairly critical. Out of surgery. They'll call me if anything changes or when he wakes up," Laurel said gently.

He'd never much appreciated gentle. Gentle tended to get trampled in this life, but Laurel's gentle was somehow steel, too, and it washed over him like a soothing balm.

"He said something to me. He said 'he didn't get it.' Then he gestured to his pocket and I pulled out a piece of paper. I read it over and tried to remember what it said. Something important."

Grady stared at the picture of the scrap of paper on Laurel's phone. He knew there was something he was supposed to remember, and it was just somewhere in the gray, frayed edges of his mind.

"You can't beat yourself up about it. I think the more you focus on trying to remember, the harder it's going to be *to* remember."

"I have an excellent memory and never forget anything. I could probably name every person who's ever walked through the doors of my bar."

"Saloon," she corrected for him, and when he glanced at her there was a hint of a smile.

He didn't have words for how badly he wanted to kiss that smile. "I'd probably remember more if you scooted a little closer."

"Grady, you have to understand that I have already put my investigation in danger because of you."

"Excuse me?"

"I don't mean that as a blame on you. It's a blame on me. For whatever reason, I have a hard time..." She looked away, clearly embarrassed and irritated with herself. "I have a hard time saying no to you. I should have put my foot down and not brought you with me."

"So you could have been shot?"

"If I'd waited with the deputies..."

"Hank could be dead. The what-ifs work both ways. Good and bad. What if-ing it is pointless, and I think you know that. You haven't compromised your investigation. Not because of me, and not because of you. Your investigation is fine. Things just aren't going easily."

"Maybe I'm used to things going easily."

"Thankfully for you, I'm not. I'll teach you."

"The thing is, Grady… Maybe there is this weird pull between us. Attraction or chemistry or, I don't know, DNA. Carsons and Delaneys forever attracted to each other like magnets only to ruin everything. But we are night and day. Opposites in every way except the one that has us working together. I am serious and permanent and all the things you avoid like the plague."

"Maybe I'm not serious about everything, but I'm serious about plenty. My family. This town. And that's permanent. I'm not all one-night stands and parties or whatever it is you think of me."

"Then what are you?" she asked, looking at him with earnest brown eyes. So earnest and pretty and, yeah, everything that wasn't usually *him*.

She was right. They should be oil and water but their Carson and Delaney roots somehow acted like soap, mixing them all together.

"Probably no good for you, princess deputy."

"It's not about being good or bad for—"

He reached over and curled his fingers around her upper arm. He was tempted to give her a good jerk, till she was sprawled out on top of him, but his body wasn't up for it. "Come over here."

"Grady—"

"Now, Laurel."

No one was more shocked than him when she obeyed.

Chapter Twelve

Laurel knew she was losing her mind, but it felt so good. Because letting Grady pull her toward him, until she was practically sprawled across half of him, felt like a relief. It cleared all the arguments in her head and released nearly all of the tension in her body.

"How often do you think you've called me by my actual name?" she asked.

"Haven't exactly kept track." He curled his finger into a strand of her hair, wrapping it around and around. "Still not going to sleep with me?"

She sighed, glancing up at the bandage on his head. "Nope."

He grinned. "Because of doctor's orders?"

She could lie. She could go back to her usual circuitous denials, but he was warm and comfortable to lean against. She didn't feel much like lying or denying or focusing. So, she told the truth. "Yes, that is why."

He pulled on the finger he'd wrapped some of her hair around, drawing her face closer to his. "Doctor's orders don't last forever."

"Maybe I don't want them to."

His eyebrows went up and she couldn't ignore the fact she got a thrill out of shocking him. Except, the thrill was immediately followed by exhaustion. "I am so tired, Grady, and I have so many things to do." So many things and all she wanted to do was rest her cheek on Grady's chest and sleep.

For a second, just one little second, she gave in to the impulse.

"Set the alarm on your phone, princess, and we'll take ourselves a little rest."

"Like this?" she asked incredulously.

Before she could explain to him that she wasn't about to take a nap curled up on top of him when he was suffering from a concussion and they weren't even...whatever it was they weren't, he'd shifted lower on the bed and they were both prone.

She was on her side, all but curled against him, her head resting on his shoulder. His arm was around her, strong and protective. She should get up. Roll away. She wasn't going to sleep with—actual sleep—with Grady. It was wholly incongruous to him and what they were or weren't and yet her eyelids were already drooping. Where it usually took her a good hour to shut up her brain and fall asleep, she already felt relaxed. Safe.

The next thing she knew her phone was jerking her out of sleep. At first she thought it was her alarm, but as she pawed on the mattress to find it, she saw the name of the hospital flashing on her screen.

She hit Accept as fast as she could, somehow all tangled up with Grady in the dark. "H-hello?" she answered breathlessly, trying to roll away from him and being caught in a hard, uncompromising grasp.

"Deputy Delaney?"

"This is her."

"Hank Gaskill is awake and doing well enough to receive very brief visits, if your questioning is absolutely necessary."

"It is. It is. I'll be there soon." She clicked End, already scooting toward the empty side of the bed so she could slide off without any physical contact with Grady. "Hank's awake. I have to go."

"We were asleep for an hour," Grady said. "You can't keep going at this pace."

She pulled on her jacket, patting herself down to make sure she had everything. "I have to. Now, can you please, *please*, call some-one?"

He sighed heavily but he held up his phone. "Ty should be around."

"Promise me you'll call him, and make sure he follows the doctor's instructions. A prom-ise, Grady. Your word."

"You think my word means anything?"

She studied his face, all sharp edges and challenge, and yet she knew what she'd always known about Grady Carson. He might be wild, he might be antagonistic and frustrating and not necessarily law-abiding, but he was not a man who went back on his word. "Yeah, I think a promise from you means something."

Something on his face altered into an ex-pression she couldn't read and wasn't sure she'd ever seen on him, at least not directed at her. "This case won't stand in our way for-ever, Laurel."

She met his gaze, and she knew he was right in the same way she knew Carsons and Del-aneys would never get along, and never leave

Bent. Even with an hour's sleep under her belt, she didn't have the energy to argue. "I know it won't. But I still have a job to do. Call Ty. I'll…check on you later."

He smiled, back to slick charm and self-satisfied humor. "I'll be waiting."

She couldn't let that mean anything. She had a job to do and a case to focus on, and Grady… Well, everything all jumbled up with him would have to wait. No matter how nice it had been to simply lie next to someone and feel safe and comfortable.

She drove back to the hospital, pushing away the exhaustion that dogged her. She'd grab a cup of coffee, then question Hank, then… She'd have to grab a few hours. The sun was just hinting at the horizon, ready to start a new day.

And you're still no closer to an answer.

So far. So far. That wasn't final.

She parked at the hospital lot and made her way up to Hank's floor. After a lot of asking around, she found his doctor.

"I don't know how lucid he'll be, and he shouldn't be agitated. So this needs to be quick and low-key. In a few days, he should be recovered enough to handle more."

Laurel nodded at the doctor before following her into the room. Hank was connected to all sorts of machines and monitors. His eyes fluttered open.

"Mr. Gaskill, this is Deputy Delaney. Do you feel well enough to answer some questions?"

"Yeah," Hank rasped. "Yeah. Did you find who did this?"

"I'm afraid not," Laurel said. "Is there anything you can tell me that would help me identify and apprehend the man who shot you?"

"I don't know who it was. It could have been someone I know. It could have been a stranger. It could have been a hit man for all I know. It was dark. Everything so dark."

Laurel eyed all the beeping machines nervously. "It's okay, Hank. You've been seriously shot. I'm going to do everything in my power to find out by who. You don't have to have all the answers."

He stilled a little. "I don't have any proof, but Adams has something to do with it. Jason was sure of it."

"Do you know why Jason met with whoever killed him?"

Hank closed his eyes, and Laurel knew she

was running out of time. This was too much for a man who'd been shot a handful of hours ago.

"He was going to blackmail the higher-up. There's someone higher up who knows, and Jason wanted to get paid to be quiet. He was going to pay me, too."

"What higher-up?"

Something beeped shrilly and the doctor moved, nudging Laurel out of the way. "Deputy, you'll need to leave. I'll alert you when he's up to a more thorough questioning."

Higher-ups and blackmail, and none of it made any sense. But she had her next step. Not sleep like she'd hoped, but Mr. Adams.

"A SHOE?"

Grady glared at Ty, who was sprawled out on a recliner in the corner. "It was hard, everything was dark, and I was a little busy knocking a gun out of his hand."

"Would have been more badass to have gotten a concussion from a gun over a shoe."

Grady scowled. "I'll keep that in mind next time I'm accosted while trying to save a man's life."

"See that you do," his cousin replied good-naturedly. "Hurt?"

"Fading," Grady lied. His head was still pounding, and every once in a while he felt sick to his stomach, but it was getting better. Maybe.

He glanced at his phone again. No updates from Laurel. It had been a little less than an hour. Plenty of time to get there and question Hank.

"A watched phone never rings from an inappropriate wannabe hookup."

Grady looked up from his phone with a doleful expression. "I'm not allowed to have an interest in this case?"

"Well, considering you said it looks like Clint is in the clear, yeah, you shouldn't. The dead Delaney wasn't anybody to you."

"That how you felt in the army? Dead guy. Not my problem."

Ty's expression went blank, and Grady regretted bringing it up. His cousin was an army ranger, had done some dangerous, amazing things in his time serving this country, and no matter how pissy Grady was, he didn't have a right to poke at that.

"Listen—"

But Ty held up his hand as his eyebrows drew together. An odd swishing sound went through the apartment, then the squeak of one of his stairs. He didn't hear footsteps, but the stairs outside didn't squeak without someone standing on them.

Grady flung the covers off his legs, but again Ty's hand stopped him. Ty moved out of the chair, cat-like and silent. When he reached the door, he picked something up off the ground. A piece of paper. His quizzical frown went furious.

He tossed it on the bed. "Be right back," he whispered.

"What the—" But Ty was already gone. Grady picked up the paper and felt as though he'd been transported into some kind of movie. Little magazine letters had been cut out and pasted onto the paper.

Watch your step and your back.

He was out of bed before he'd made it to the last word, but by the time he pulled on his boots, Ty was back.

"Gone," Ty muttered in disgust. "Someone must have been waiting. Though I didn't hear a car, which I would have." Ty shook his head.

"I imagine this is about Delaney's case and not some wronged ex-lover."

"I imagine," Grady returned.

Ty sighed heavily. "Call your little deputy, Grady. If this is about the case, she needs to know."

Part of him wanted to leave her out of it. He could handle whatever coward thought he could intimidate a Carson, but it *did* have to do with the case, undoubtedly, which meant there might be a clue.

He grabbed his phone and pulled up Laurel's number. When she answered, she sounded exhausted and pissed.

"Grady—"

"I received a little message under my door about ten minutes ago."

"A message?"

"I'm afraid you're going to need to come check it out."

"Is this a joke? Because—"

Grady held out the phone to Ty. "Would you tell her?"

Ty rolled his eyes but took the outstretched phone. "Delaney? Ty. Stop being difficult and come do your job, huh?"

It was Grady's turn to roll *his* eyes. "Charming as ever," he noted, grabbing the phone back. "Laur—" But the call had ended.

"Does it always have to be antagonism?" Grady demanded of Ty.

"To a Delaney? Yeah, I'm pretty sure that's how it works."

"It doesn't have to work that way. Did it ever occur to you that the people who fed us all that feud garbage weren't exactly good people?"

Ty's eyes widened. "You slept with her."

"No, I haven't," Grady returned, irritable and edgy. "But I am thirty-three years old and playing cops and robbers is getting old. My dad was a miserable SOB. My mom wasn't much better. Blaming the Delaneys for everything wrong in their lives never got them anywhere but more miserable."

"Sometimes the Delaneys *are* the source of a person's misery, and before you start reading into *that*, let me just say that if you're letting some woman convince you everything our entire family, and lives, and town are built on is crap, then maybe you need to get a hold of yourself."

"Maybe I don't want my life to be built on a feud that's older than my saloon."

"Then you aren't the Grady Carson I know, and I'm not sure one I want to."

Grady clenched and unclenched his jaw, enough unspent fury pumping through him he wouldn't mind a little bit of a fight. Except he had a concussion and he *was* tired. Tired of fighting and feuds and things that only existed because they always had.

He still believed in Bent and history, but he wasn't a boy playing at a man anymore, and he wasn't going to let history or this town dictate how he lived his life.

"Guess you can go, then."

"Guess I will," Ty replied, grabbing his coat and striding out the door.

Grady gave in to the impulse to slam his hand against the wall, and immediately regretted the way it jarred his head.

When Laurel finally made it back, she didn't knock or even pause. She barged right into his apartment. She looked around, frowning.

"Where's Ty?"

"Left."

She fisted her hands on her hips. "He was supposed to take care of you."

"Yeah, well, he was being an ass. So I booted

him. Now, are you here to do police work or what?" He handed her the paper.

She read, her expression going flat and hard, and Grady wasn't surprised to see some mean-edged cop on her, or the fact it turned him on. But she also had dark circles under her eyes and her usually creamy complexion was near gray.

"You're going to crash, princess."

"Sooner or later," she agreed, frowning at the paper. "I don't like this."

"Can't say I care for it, either."

"You can't be alone. Not until we figure this out."

He offered her a smile. "You going to play bodyguard?"

"I have an investigation to run."

"I can help."

"I'm going to take you to the Carson Ranch. There's enough of you to keep an eye on things."

"On a big spread like ours? I'm not taking this to the ranch and potentially endangering my family. You want me not alone, you're up. Since you're already involved."

He could tell she wanted to argue, but in the end, she nodded. "Unfortunately, you're right."

"Well, now, those are words I never thought I'd hear from you. 'Unfortunately' notwithstanding."

"But there are conditions."

"Of course there are."

"You go where I go, not the other way around. You listen to me. You *obey* me. Because this isn't a joke, and it isn't a game. I have a ticking time bomb of an investigation, more and more people in danger by the second. You're going to have to swallow your Wyoming-sized pride and do what I tell you to do."

Grady gave her a grand mock salute, but she didn't even crack a smile.

"I don't want anything to happen to you," she said in that earnest way that made him feel something close to *vulnerable*. Which was crap.

"Get it through your head that the same goes, okay?"

She sighed. "Well, let's get going, then."

"Where are we off to?"

"We have to question a possible suspect."

"Please tell me it's not my brother. Or any Carson."

Laurel quirked a tiny smile at that. "It's your

lucky day. This suspect is as Carson-free as you can get."

"So, he's a Delaney?"

"Worse. An outsider."

Chapter Thirteen

It wasn't easy to pretend the warning letter to Grady didn't rattle her, but she knew she needed to present the tough cop facade right now. Not just because Grady was now under her protection, no matter how laughable that seemed, but also because she had to face Mr. Adams in a professional, smart way that hopefully led to a confession or more of a lead.

It was hard to believe the pudgy, middle-aged manager of an unassuming mine could be a cold-blooded killer, strong enough to hit Grady so hard with a *shoe* it gave him a concussion, and agile enough to slip through darkened woods and out again without getting caught.

But she couldn't rule it out, either.

The town of Clearwater was quite a bit larger than Bent. Many of the nonlocal mine workers lived here, so there was a sprawling residential area. Since the town had sprung out of meeting the needs of those workers, everything was more modern than Bent. Fast food, a Walmart, even stoplights.

"How much you want to bet this guy lives in the nicest house in town?" Grady asked, clearly not impressed.

"Well, he is the mine manager."

Grady made a rude noise. "You think this guy is the one who knocked me out?"

"No," Laurel said firmly, turning onto the street Mr. Adams lived on. "But he's involved. Now, we need to go over a few procedure ground rules."

"Of course we do."

Laurel ignored the sarcasm. "You can't go in with me."

"I thought I was under your protection, Deputy," Grady returned, all mock innocence.

"It's tricky and it's complicated, but I can't have you shooting off at the mouth. It will call into question my investigation and if there is a trial, and Mr. Adams is accused of some wrongdoing, your presence and interference will be noted and used to undermine everything. I can't risk it."

Grady was silent as she pulled to a stop in front of the Adams residence. She turned to him, surprised when he hadn't mounted an argument, but also not convinced he would listen to her. When did he ever listen to her?

"Stay put. For the sake of making a murderer, and possibly his accomplice, *pay*."

"What about a little creative use of the truth?"

Laurel frowned, but he had said truth, and Grady might be all manner of wild, rule-breaking things, but he tended to dwell in the truth of it all. "I'm listening."

"We'll say I'm looking for Clint, since we know he's been hanging out with Lizzie. He's not here, I say fine. Then you can question Mr. Adams in a separate room and I can quietly and patiently wait."

"You can't snoop."

Grady grinned. "I can't snoop and tell you about it, but I can snoop for my own peace of mind." He put a hand to his heart. "My brother could be missing."

"And is more likely at the Carson Ranch sleeping off teenage idiocy."

"More than likely, but you never know. Might as well give it a shot."

Laurel blew out a breath. She didn't know if it was genius or stupid and that was always the problem with Grady. He obscured both with those sinful smiles and mischievous glances.

"It's like having a partnership with mayhem," Laurel muttered, pushing out of the car.

"I'll take that as a compliment *and* agreement."

They walked up the well-kept path to the door side by side. Laurel reached out and pushed the doorbell as Grady surveyed the yard and house.

"I was right about the nicest house in town," Grady mumbled as Mr. Adams slowly pulled the door open.

His eyebrows were furrowed and he was clearly surprised and concerned to see her. "Uh, Deputy. I'm sorry, I don't recall your name..."

"Deputy Delaney. Mr. Adams, do you have a few moments to answer some questions for me?"

Mr. Adams looked nervously from Laurel to Grady's bandage and back to Laurel. "Erm, I suppose. Is...is something the matter?"

"We hope not. I have a few more questions about the Jason Delaney murder case, and Mr.

Carson here is looking for his missing brother, who was last seen with your daughter."

Mr. Adams blinked at that. "I don't know anyone named Carson."

"His last name is Danvers. Clint Danvers," Grady supplied, and Laurel was quite impressed with how concerned brother he sounded.

"Oh, Clint. Yes, he and Lizzie have been working on a school project together."

Laurel did her best not to snort. She'd have almost felt bad for the guy for being so clueless if it wasn't for the fact he might be linked to murder.

"I haven't seen him in a while, and I have to say I'm starting to get awfully worried. I don't suppose Lizzie is around so I could ask her if she knows where he is."

Mr. Adams blinked in surprise and clearly balked at the request, so Laurel fixed her kindest smile on her face.

"If you'd feel more comfortable with a woman asking her, I can do it."

"Why don't I go get her and we'll… We'll all discuss it together." Mr. Adams smiled thinly. "She's in her room."

"Do you mind if I come with? I have

some—" she glanced at Grady, then back at Mr. Adams "—confidential questions I'd like to ask you."

"Oh. Oh. Well, I suppose."

Laurel followed Mr. Adams from the entryway toward a staircase. She glanced back at Grady, who was whistling as he wandered the large entryway. She wanted to roll her eyes, but instead she focused on Mr. Adams.

She had to consider her words carefully. Hank's not-quite-clear answers didn't give her specifics to go on, so she had to fill in some blanks and hope she was right. "Were you aware Jason Delaney had evidence something criminal was going on at the mine, and was threatening to blackmail a higher-level official within the company?"

Mr. Adams stopped in his tracks. He looked genuinely surprised, but his next question left Laurel more than a little suspicious.

"How do you know that?"

She smiled apologetically. "I'm not at liberty to say."

"I… I had no idea." Mr. Adams resumed his pace up the stairs, but Laurel noted he'd gone pale.

"There's some concern you could be involved, Mr. Adams."

Again he paused, this time at the top of the stairs. He licked his lips, looking around nervously. "Involved… I… I didn't know… I…" He cleared his throat. "You've caught me quite by surprise."

"Clearly." Though Laurel didn't know if it was the right kind of surprise. "Please understand, I have to do my due diligence, and I hope if you know anything at all, you'll pass it along to the police. It's always so much worse on someone when they try to hide the truth."

He was all but sweating now, swallowing nearly convulsively as he reached out for a doorknob.

"This is Lizzie's room," he said, his hand shaking, his voice weak. When he tried to turn the knob, he frowned. "Locked. How odd." He knocked on the door. "Lizzie. Are you awake? I'm afraid I need you to come talk to some people for me." He chuckled weakly and looked at Laurel. "Teenagers do love their sleeping in."

"Mr. Adams. If you don't answer my questions in a forthright manner, I will be forced to investigate you further. Not just for whatever criminal activity is happening at the mine, but the murder of Jason Delaney, as well as attempted murder of an unnamed victim and the attack on another man. Do you understand?"

Mr. Adams nodded, jiggling the doorknob desperately. "Of course, Deputy. I don't know a thing about any of those things. I swear."

That Laurel didn't believe for a second, but the door swung open and a young, blonde teen answered, flushed and nervous-looking. "Hi, Daddy." She gulped. "Who's this?"

"The police, sweetheart. They're looking for your school friend Clint."

Lizzie's eyes widened at Laurel. "Clint?" she squeaked. "Uh, why?"

Laurel noted a boy's boot was partly visible, as though someone had attempted to shove it under the bed, along with a pair of men's jeans crumpled on one side of the room. Laurel decided to go for a little creative truth herself.

"His brother's been injured and—"

A rustling sounded and Clint tumbled out of the closet. "Grady's been hurt?" he demanded.

Mr. Adams made an outraged, choking sound.

"Grab your pants and head downstairs," Laurel said, stepping between the fuming Mr.

Adams and the half-dressed teen. "I suggest you hurry."

Clint scrambled to gather his clothes and darted out the door while Laurel stood in front of Mr. Adams. When he made a move for the boy, Laurel put her hand out.

"Let's all calm down now."

"You little slut!" Mr. Adams shouted.

The poor girl began to cry and Laurel wasn't exactly gentle pulling Mr. Adams out of the room. "I suggest you calm yourself."

But he pushed her away, heading for the stairs Clint had just run down. "I want him arrested! This instant!"

"Your daughter is eighteen. There's nothing arrest-worthy happening here. Now, if you would stop—"

Clint skidded to a stop in front of Grady.

"What are you doing here?" they asked each other in unison.

"You're not that hurt," Clint said, frowning at Grady's bandage.

"But apparently you're that dumb," Grady muttered in return, glancing up at the furious Mr. Adams.

Clint quickly shoved his legs into his jeans,

then his feet into the boots he'd been carrying. "I gotta go."

Laurel took the moment of surprise and confusion to move past Mr. Adams on the staircase. "Let him go," she mouthed to Grady, nodding at Clint.

Grady moved out of the way of Clint's escape, but he stepped side by side with Laurel to block Mr. Adams from him as Clint slipped out the door.

"He... He defiled my daughter!" Mr. Adams shouted, pointing at Clint's retreating form, his face growing redder and redder.

Grady raised an eyebrow. "Seriously?"

"Mr. Adams," Laurel said as calmly as she could manage. "Your daughter is eighteen. And upset by your behavior. You should calm yourself and have a civil conversation with her."

Mr. Adams poked his finger wildly at her "I don't need *you* telling me how to handle my daughter."

"Clearly," Laurel replied sarcastically before she could bite back the response. She forced herself to retrieve a card from her pocket. "If you have any further information you'd like to divulge on the mine, Jason Delaney, et cetera, please give me a call."

Mr. Adams stared at the card, but seemed to regather his wits and took it. "I assure you, I know nothing about any of that."

Laurel nodded. "I hope my investigation reflects that, for your sake." Laurel turned for the door, ushering Grady out.

"That asshole is lying," Grady said flatly.

"Through his teeth," Laurel agreed, pulling her phone out of her pocket. "I need search warrants ASAP."

"How long is that going to take?"

A question she didn't want to answer. "Long enough for him to tip off whoever's got a hold on him."

"What about the girl? You think she might know something?"

"Maybe. Maybe." Laurel slid into her car and waited for Grady to get in the passenger side. "We'll go to the station so I can apply for the search warrant. Then... Why don't you call Clint? See if he can get Lizzie to come over for dinner at the Carson Ranch."

"Dinner?" Grady asked.

"Get her there under the guise of meeting Clint's family. Get her away from her father and in a neutral, safe space, and she might feel comfortable enough to talk. Maybe she doesn't know anything, but if she does I doubt she's going to tell me under her father's roof, and I don't want to drag a young girl into the police station if I don't have to."

"And that's legal?"

Laurel shrugged. "Depends on what she says. If I have to go the straight and narrow route with the search warrant, I can get a little creative in the questioning department."

"My, my, my, Deputy Delaney, you are full of surprises."

"Don't you forget it."

GRADY HAD SPENT more than his fair share of minutes trying to rile Laurel up, but watching her reaction to the judge denying her search warrant application was like nothing he'd ever seen.

She swore admirably. She fumed. She ranted as she drove from the sheriff's department all the way to the Carson Ranch.

"I don't think I've ever been more turned on," he offered once she took a breath.

"Oh, shut up," she returned, wholly unamused. Which, admittedly, served to amuse *him* more.

"Still no word from Clint?" she asked irritably.

"Not since he picked Lizzie up. They should beat us here, though."

She shook her head. "Something doesn't feel right. Something is off. I'm *missing* something."

"Then we'll find it."

She took a deep breath and let it out, straightening her shoulders as she drove up the bumpy, curving drive to the main house.

He liked that he'd calmed her some, and wished he could feel it inside of himself, but mostly he felt the same way she did. Something didn't feel right, and he didn't know what.

"You have to deal with this every case?"

"Deal with what?"

"That dogged not knowing what is going on?"

"Not every case, but some. A lot of not knowing is part of the job."

"Your job blows."

Her mouth curved. "It's not such a bad thing, putting it all together, knowing you can."

"Well, if you know you can, you can. So, you should stop ranting."

"I thought it turned you on."

Grady chuckled, but it died when they reached the house. "He's not here."

"He could have parked in one of the outbuildings, couldn't he?"

"Could have, but wouldn't." Clint wasn't that thorough. Grady shaded his eyes against the setting sun and looked around the property before turning his attention back to Laurel. "We should head back into town. Retrace what would have been his steps. They might have stopped somewhere to make out or something, but…"

"But maybe not. Is Ty in town?" she asked, already reversing the car and heading back the way they'd come. "We could split up our search and meet in the middle."

"Good thinking." Grady sent a quick message off to Ty as Laurel sped down the drive they'd just ambled up. Her gaze was shrewd on the road, hands grasped tight on the steering wheel, and it was an odd thing to not be in charge and not have it grate.

But his little brother might be in trouble and

there wasn't a lot of room for any other emotions above fear.

"Keep your eyes peeled and tell me if you see anything," Laurel said. But as they drove, all he saw was road and the expanse of a Wyoming landscape.

"He's dead to me," Grady muttered, pissed off beyond belief the way fear gripped him. But he'd been attacked and threatened, a man had been killed, and now his brother was nowhere.

"Keep trying his cell," Laurel instructed calmly.

Anyone else's calmness in this situation would have only served to stoke his irritation higher, but something about Laurel's no-nonsense approach and the clear seriousness she took this with soothed rather than rattled.

"Let's stop at the gas station, see if anyone noticed anything. Ty should be catching up with us soon."

"Okay."

Laurel pulled into the gas station's parking lot and pushed her door open, but she glanced at him before she stepped out. She reached over, squeezed his forearm. "We'll find him. We will."

He took in those serious brown eyes and the determined set of her jaw and he nodded, some of that panic settling into something a lot more peaceful.

He stepped out with her and heard his name shouted. Clint burst from the front door of the station, blood dripping down his face. "Grady!"

Grady grabbed his brother, trying to figure out why he had blood all over him. He opened his mouth to demand answers, but Clint was already talking.

"Someone grabbed her. Just…grabbed her." He turned to Laurel, all heavy breathing and fear and desperation. "You gotta find her."

"Did you call the police?" Laurel asked composedly, though her whole body had tensed next to his.

"You are the police!"

Laurel didn't respond to that, but immediately began speaking in low tones into her radio.

"What was she wearing?" Laurel asked.

"Uh. Jeans. A T-shirt. Pink, I think. Pinkish. She had my jacket on. Leather jacket."

"What can you tell me about the car?" Laurel asked gently.

Clint swallowed, tears clearly swimming in his eyes. "Black. Slick." Clint rattled off a few possible makes and models. "The plate wasn't Wyoming. It was yellow, I think. Yellowish or something close."

Laurel relayed the information into her radio as Ty roared into the gas station, screeching to a halt on his motorcycle in front of them. "What's going on?"

"We need to get him to a hospital," Grady said roughly.

"No way, man. I have to find her."

"That gash is nasty. You need stitches. Did you lose consciousness?"

"No, I'm fine. They just knocked me down and I hit my head. He was gone by the time I got back up."

"Did Lizzie know the man who took her?" Laurel interjected.

"No! He had a ski mask thing on. I was gassing up and he just got out of his car and pushed me down and grabbed her. It took me a minute to get up and he shoved her in the car and left."

"He knocked you out."

"Whatever, man," Clint replied, pushing

Grady's concerned hand away. "We have to find her. We have to."

"We've got a lot to go on. Write anything else you can think of down, okay? Ty, you take him to the hospital. I'll send an officer to watch and take Clint's statement."

"And what are we doing?" Grady asked.

"This time, we're getting consent to search Adams's house without having to wait around for a search warrant." She stopped midstep toward the car and then turned to him. "I mean, you don't have to come with me. I've given Lizzie's name and description to county, and I've sent the closest officer to the hospital to question Clint. You'd be safe there, if you want to be with Clint. I'd under—"

"I'll be safe with you, too. Let's go."

Chapter Fourteen

Laurel knocked on Mr. Adams's door for the second time in two days. When Mr. Adams opened the door, his face was red, his thinning hair wild. "Did you find her? Is she—"

"Mr. Adams, I need consent to search your house. We're looking for any clues that might help us find Lizzie."

"My…consent." The man choked on something like a sob, but Laurel couldn't let that sway her. "My daughter is missing."

"Yes, and the Bent County Sheriff's Department is doing everything in their power to find her. Including this. If you give us consent, Deputy Hart and I will search the entire house." Laurel nodded at Hart, who was standing behind her. "We'll take anything that might aid us in finding her whereabouts."

"I…" Mr. Adams raked his shaking hands

through his hair. "All right. You can search the house."

"Sign this, please." Laurel nodded to Hart, who held out the consent form. With shaking hands, Mr. Adams signed it.

"If you'd leave the door open while we search, and find somewhere out of the way to be." She glanced back at Grady, whom she'd instructed to stay in the car.

He, of course, wasn't *in* the car, but leaning against it, looking somehow lazy and lethal at the same time, the stitches on his head adding to the dangerous vibe. She sighed heavily. She didn't like leaving him out there, but there weren't a lot of choices right now.

"I… You…" Mr. Adams made another choking sound, but he finally got out of the way of the door.

"Upstairs. First door on your left," Laurel directed Hart.

Laurel herself headed through the lower level of the house while Mr. Adams trailed after her, sputtering ineffectively. What she wanted to find was some kind of home office or place where he'd have things related to work. "I don't suppose you have any information as to who might have taken your daughter, or why."

"Miss Delaney, I don't know who's responsible," Mr. Adams rasped.

"If you say so," she returned evenly, ignoring the Miss instead of Deputy.

"No, I mean, I don't know their name or anything to identify them by. The man I've been working for is a nameless, faceless entity. I get messages, and I act on them. I don't keep my job if I don't act on them."

Laurel whirled on the admission. "So this has something to do with the mine?"

Mr. Adams sank into a chair, rubbing his hands over his face. "Yes. I guess. I was just told to get rid of some papers. To cover some things up. When Jason started poking around..." He looked up at her plaintively. "I didn't kill him. I don't have anything to do with this except paperwork."

"I need to know everything about the paperwork. I need a list of anyone who is above you and would be affected if the information you destroyed got out. I need everything you know, Mr. Adams. For Lizzie's sake."

He swallowed audibly and nodded. "My office is upstairs. I don't have anything specific, but I can write down some things. They took Lizzie because she's been..." His voice broke and he cleared his throat. "I don't know why, but she's been poking around my work. Asking me questions about the mine, about Jason, and I didn't know what was going on. I figured she'd get bored of it, but—"

"Delaney," Hart called from above. "I found a license plate number written on a scrap of paper."

Laurel met Hart at the bottom of the stairs, glancing at the looping scrawl of what had to be a license plate number.

"Call it in. Have someone check it out," she said.

Hart nodded and started talking into his radio.

Laurel turned her attention to the man behind her. A man who'd clearly done some illegal things, but was scared sick by his daughter's disappearance and his worry for her.

"Show me your office."

He started walking and she followed him up the stairs while Hart stood in the entryway, relaying his information to dispatch.

Mr. Adams led her to a small room at the end of the hall. It was nicely decorated, dominated by a huge desk. There was a recliner in the corner and everything was neat as a pin.

"I don't bring anything home, and everything I was told to destroy, I destroyed, but I… Lately I've been getting nervous, what with the murder and all, so I started keeping a list." With shaking hands, Mr. Adams opened up a drawer, then reached toward the back, popping something that turned out to be a false bottom.

But instead of a piece of paper or anything innocent, there was a gun. Clear as day. Mr. Adams gasped.

"It isn't mine," he whispered, his voice sounding strained. "I don't own a gun. I don't."

Laurel pulled rubber gloves out of her utility belt and put them on. She picked up the weapon. It was exactly the kind of gun that could have killed Jason Delaney. She closed her eyes for a minute because she wasn't stupid.

Mr. Adams wasn't the murderer, but someone sure wanted her to think he was.

"My notes. They're gone," Mr. Adams gasped, pawing around the false bottom. But it was empty save for the gun. "Oh, God. Oh, God."

"Hart," Laurel barked.

After a few seconds, the deputy appeared. His eyes widened when he saw what Laurel was holding.

"I need you to run the serial number on this gun." She rattled it off to him and Hart relayed the number to dispatch. She racked her brain for a reason to take in Mr. Adams so they could have him in custody while they ran ballistics on the weapon, because as long as his daughter wasn't safe, neither was he. Neither were Clint and Hank, for that matter.

The radio squawked and everyone in the room heard the results clear as day. "That gun has been reported as stolen."

Laurel glanced at Mr. Adams, who looked panic-stricken. "Stolen? I don't own a gun. I haven't stolen a gun. That isn't mine! My notes are gone!"

"Hart. Arrest him."

"No. No! I didn't do anything. Please, understand. I didn't… They're making this…"

"Mr. Adams," Laurel began firmly so he'd stop blubbering and listen. "You have a stolen weapon in your home. I have to arrest you. We'll need to run ballistics on it, and if it comes back as the murder weapon in the Jason Delaney case—"

"What have I done? Oh, God." Mr. Adams began to cry, and Laurel almost felt sympathy for the man, but he'd gotten himself mixed up in some ugly business.

"Consider this the best thing for you right now, Mr. Adams. You'll be safe, and this might be leverage we can use to get Lizzie released. If whoever has her is worried about being linked to the murder, having someone arrested for it might lower their guard. If it's the murder weapon."

He calmed a little bit at that.

"Hart, I want you to arrest him and take him to the station, and get a recording of everything he can remember about the documents he destroyed. Along with anyone he might want to implicate."

Hart stepped forward and went through the steps to arrest Mr. Adams while Laurel continued to look through all the drawers. She sat down at the desk as Hart led Mr. Adams away. She didn't know what she was looking for, but she could confiscate the computer along with the murder weapon.

She wasn't sure she believed Mr. Adams was completely ignorant of who was behind all of this, but a trip to the station and videotaped questioning might help jog his memory. If nothing else, she truly believed it would convince the real killer they weren't still looking for him.

"I thought we decided he wasn't the murderer."

Laurel glanced over her shoulder to find Grady taking up the entire doorway. "You shouldn't be in here," she said, though the words were a waste and she knew it. "I don't think he's the murderer, but someone wants us to think he is. I don't have any proof he's *not* the murderer. A stolen weapon in the house is enough to bring him in."

She turned back to the desk. "I have to search everything. Once I'm done, and I've compiled all the evidence I've found, we'll drop it off at the station, then head over to the hospital and see if Clint remembers anything."

"You have to sleep at some point, princess."

Her shoulders slumped and the wave of exhaustion she'd been fighting off with sheer adrenaline threatened to topple her. "Yeah, at some point. But not yet." A few more steps and then she could think about sleep.

Grady's large hand covered her shoulder, squeezed. She looked up at him with a million snippy responses she knew she needed to give him. But all she wanted to do was lean into him. Rest against him.

Which wasn't something she could allow herself. "Wait downstairs. Don't touch anything. I'll be down as soon as I'm done."

He didn't remove his hand. Instead, the other came up and cradled her cheek, gentle as could be. Something like a lump lodged itself in her throat at the sheer *wanting*. Wanting him. Wanting sleep. Wanting to just *rest*.

"I'll go downstairs. You've got half an hour to finish up. Then you'll drop off anything you need to at the station. After that, you're heading straight for bed."

"Is that an order?"

He grinned that horrible, lust-inducing grin. "Yeah, I think it is."

It was the simply *kind*, almost caring way he said it that made the lump in her throat impossible to swallow. "Decided you're my caretaker now?" she asked through a tight throat.

"I think we mutually decided that for each other. Get to work, Deputy. I'm tired, too."

On a deep breath, Laurel pulled out of the grasp of Grady's rough hands and did just that.

GRADY'D HAD HIS fill of waiting for people. He'd also had his fill of Laurel looking like she was about to keel over, and then pressing forward as if her sheer force of will could keep her awake for years.

Hell, maybe it could. She walked out of the sheriff's department looking with-it and strong no matter that legions of shadows existed under her eyes. So much so he could see them even in the parking lot lights.

"How's Clint?" she asked.

"Hospital released him. Ty's taking him back to the ranch and him, Noah and Vanessa will keep him out of trouble. I gave him your number in case he remembers something important."

She nodded. "Good."

He hopped off the hood of her car, where he'd been sitting and waiting. "I'm driving."

She rolled her eyes. "You can't drive my county-issued vehicle, Carson."

"Why not?"

"It's against the law. Plus, you've had a concussion."

"I believe that was something like twenty-four hours ago. Which means I'm okay to drive now."

"God, has it been twenty-four hours?" She raked her hands through her hair, which had come out of its band at some point between finding Clint and now.

"Heck of a twenty-four hours."

She huffed out something close to a laugh. "I suppose." She pulled her keys out of her pocket. "If anyone asks, you put a gun to my head before I let you drive my car."

"Got it." He took her keys, trying to tone down his self-satisfied smirk a *little* bit.

She slid into the passenger seat, her eyes already drooping, and he turned the keys in the ignition.

He didn't bother to talk. He let her lean against the window by her side as he drove them away from the sheriff's department and toward Bent. The long way. Because he had a bad feeling that wherever he stopped, she'd pop back up into Deputy Delaney mode and never get any real rest.

So he drove through the glittering late night, enjoying the peace and the stars, and only finally heading to Laurel's place when he started to come perilously close to dozing off himself.

As he drove Laurel's car up the smooth, curving drive that led to her cabin on the fancy

Delaney spread, he couldn't help wondering at this *thing* inside of him.

He'd been bred to hate Delaneys. Told stories of their wrongdoings over the centuries. He'd reveled in that. Being the underdogs, the dangerous ones. He'd used it to excuse the things he'd wanted to excuse in his life.

But Laurel had never fit with all that fiction he'd allowed himself. Something vibrant and good with this odd tug between them he'd always known was there, but had sought to avoid.

But there was no more avoiding. It was here, stronger with every passing hour as they tried to solve this mystery together. The fact of the matter was, a fact he wouldn't likely admit to anyone possibly ever, he cared about Laurel Delaney.

Not just attraction, or that teenaged desire of something that was off-limits and too good for him besides. Not just this lifetime of a wait, the anticipation, the holding himself back since he was a kid and believing he could control that tug.

This was more, and that was what had made the wait endure all those years. That he knew her and understood her. That he *liked* her. That her work ethic made *his* pale in comparison and he'd never met anyone who'd come close.

He parked on the little square of gravel and looked over at her sleeping form in the dim glow of moon and starlight filtered through the car windows.

Even as his body hardened, because she was gorgeous, his heart did some painful twisting thing. That care lodged far too deep to ignore anymore, to avoid, and he was very afraid burrowed too deep to ever be mined out.

"Wake up, princess, or I'm going to have to heft you over my shoulder," he said, far too gruffly. Because truth be told, he didn't know how to do care without a lot of gruff to cover it up. To hide the softness. Ward off the inevitable attack. Wasn't that what dear old Dad had taught him?

Laurel blinked her eyes open, staring out the windshield and then at him. "Oh. You brought me home." She frowned at the clock. "That was a heck of a drive."

"I figured it ensured you at least got an hour."

She pushed out of the car into the frigid night air and took a deep breath. "Feel like a new woman." She grinned over the hood of the car at him. "Now I don't need to sleep at all." But that confidence was underscored when she yawned.

"Uh-huh," he replied, rifling through her keys until he found one that looked like a house key. He tried it in the lock and it worked.

She stepped inside, yawning again as she flipped on a light. When she turned to face him, she frowned.

"Where are you going?"

"To the saloon."

"You can't be alone. You really can't be alone in my car."

"What do you suggest, then?" It was something of a challenge, one he probably shouldn't have laid down when they were both exhausted and no real breaks in the case had been made.

Her gaze held his, unwavering and potent, that thing always between them crackling with a new kind of electricity. Because they'd both acknowledged it now, because they were both operating on less than full capacity. Or just because it was *time*.

"I guess I suggest the inevitable," she said quietly, yet in that self-possessed, certain way she said everything. She stepped forward, as if she had no doubts or concerns, and slid her arms around his neck.

"Is that what it is?" he asked, his voice a rough rasp as she stared up at him, her mouth parted and *right there*. "Inevitable?"

"It feels that way," she replied, her tall, lithe body pressing to his, those brown eyes never leaving his gaze. As if one hour of sleep had given her all the power she needed. "But maybe I just want to." Then her mouth slid against his, soft and hot.

It felt like centuries of waiting even though he'd just kissed her the other day. Her mouth insistent, determined, so *her*, and he wanted to taste every contour of it until it was etched in his very bones.

He didn't seem to be alone in that desire. Her tongue moved against his, her arms clamped around his neck as if she could keep him there, devouring her mouth.

More, his mind chanted. *More, more, more.*

"Grady, I *want* you," she murmured against his mouth. "Now."

He kicked the door behind them closed before moving her toward her bedroom, their arms still wrapped around each other.

"Consider it me taking advantage of your

exhaustion," he gritted out, backing her toward the bed. "Then you can pretend you regret it in the morning."

"I won't." She met his gaze then, her brown eyes dark and serious. "I won't." She pulled his mouth back to hers as they tumbled onto the bed together.

Chapter Fifteen

Laurel had never been all that concerned with sex before. When she was in a relationship, it was nice to have, certainly. A kind of physical comfort, two bodies coming together.

There was nothing easy or particularly comfortable about Grady on top of her, pushing her into her mattress, his mouth unrelenting and perfect against hers, his hands molding to every curve of her body as if he couldn't stop himself. Not because it hurt or she was in an awkward position, but because there was this desperate ache inside of her, growing and growing without getting any closer to being fulfilled.

This was not the precursor to sex she knew. This was wild and desperate and she felt like if she didn't feel Grady's naked skin against hers and soon, she might simply combust and turn to ash. Or, worse, beg.

She could feel his erection against the apex of her thighs and it made her wonder if all the minimal sex she'd been having in her life had just been bad. Or if not bad, adequate. Decent and all, but not…this all-encompassing, reason-killing thing.

She pawed at his shirt, wanting to see the grand expanse of his chest, wanting to feel it under her fingertips or pressed against her body.

She'd had a lifetime of occasionally catching glimpses of Grady without a shirt on, but here in her bedroom, in her *bed*, it was, well, it was something else as he sat up and pulled off his T-shirt.

She could see every fine line of his tattoo that took up most of his shoulder and weaved its way down to his elbow. She could reach out and touch the delineation of each impressive muscle, and she could truly absorb and enjoy just how *big* he was. She didn't have to fight that or prove she was just as strong or could take him down. She didn't have to be Deputy Delaney here. For a little while she could just be Laurel.

He reached out and jerked her shirt off her in one quick pull. There was a jolt of self-consciousness that lasted all of five seconds, because his gaze was hot and blazing on her as if he could eat her alive.

She could recognize it in him, because she felt the same way, and that was the thing about whatever it was that existed between them. Maybe it had never made sense, and they'd certainly both ignored and avoided it, but they had always both *felt* it.

He reached forward and palmed her breasts, still clad in her bra, but then he jerked the bra down, not even bothering with the clasp. His hands rasping against the sensitive skin there as his mouth descended onto her mouth, kissing down her neck to her breasts. His beard scraped against her skin everywhere he kissed. It was abrasive and harsh and somehow that made every feeling deep inside of her sparkle brighter and higher.

Abruptly, Grady's mouth left her and he got off the bed. She tried to formulate a question, but she was breathing too hard as he yanked his phone out of his pocket and tossed it as if he didn't care if it landed on a hard surface and broke apart. His keys were next, but when he got his wallet, he flipped it open and pulled out a condom.

She exhaled harshly and maybe she should have been put off by the fact he had a condom, but she didn't care. She flat-out didn't care how or why or how long, as long as he used it with her.

"Take off your pants," he ordered.

Laurel gladly scrambled to comply as he undid the button and zipper on his own pants. As she kicked off her khakis and her underwear, she watched all of Grady come into view. Everything about him strong and broad and beautiful.

There was some dim part of her mind reminding her this was Grady Carson and she wasn't supposed to be getting involved with him. Certainly not like this.

But every other part of her didn't care. Because Grady, for all his swagger and outward appearance and sarcastic jokes, was good and kind and he might not want to ever admit it, but he cared about her. The same way she cared about him. An indelible fact they'd both spent too long trying to falsify.

He was standing there at the foot of her bed, completely naked and impressive. She sat on her bed, naked save for the bra he'd pushed down to her waist.

He flicked a glance at it. "Get it off."

She didn't even hesitate to do as he demanded. To do anything he demanded. Because she had always been in charge in life. She'd never cared for following anyone else's moral compass or rules. She had her own strident ones. She knew how she wanted to live her life, and she did it. Always.

But she'd never felt wild. She'd never been consumed by need or desire, and so why not follow his every order? He was the expert after all.

Grady put one knee on the bed, looming like an incredibly sexy conqueror. She would gladly be conquered. Exhaustion and feuds be damned. All she wanted in this moment was Grady.

He opened the condom wrapper, rolling on the latex before covering her body with his. And she was completely covered. Being flattened into her mattress was a delicious feeling. To live in this world that was only Grady, hard and hot and demanding on top of her.

His hands explored her body, and she smoothed her hands down his expansive, smooth back. His mouth nuzzled against the curve of her neck until she was sighing with pleasure, arching herself against him, desperate for him to enter. Her body somehow both relaxed and coiled at the same moment.

When he finally slid inside of her, there was a moment where they both paused. Holding on to each other, watching each other. Connected. As though she could see over a century in his eyes and vice versa.

Inevitable. That word kept repeating itself in her mind. Because this felt nothing short of inevitable. This was where she belonged. He was everything she needed. She didn't believe in feuds. She didn't believe in curses of Carsons and Delaneys commingling. But she understood in this moment it was not for the faint of heart. This joining, this meeting. It was only for those strong enough to handle it.

It was a very lucky thing she was strong enough. And so was he.

Grady surged inside of her in a long, slow, inexorable glide as if he felt it, too. The inevitability. The strength it would take and how much they were made for it.

His mouth claimed hers as he moved against her, over and over again, bringing her to a blinding kind of climax she'd never experienced before, shattering around him and chanting his name as he brought her to that peak again.

Her name from his lips against her mouth as together they tumbled off the edge of something that felt nothing short of perfect and meant to be.

GRADY FIGURED HE must be dreaming when a repeatedly shrill noise sounded and he was all wrapped up in a very naked Laurel. Surely this was an alternate universe he found himself in. Because there was no way the things he remembered from the night before could be real. Just no possible way.

In this dream, she was as perfect as he might have imagined. And in this dream, it felt as though no possible outcome of his life could be anything other than Laurel in it. In his bed. Always.

Yes, it had to be a dream.

But Laurel's sleepy voice was very real as it murmured a hello next to him. Her warm and very naked body next to him making him instantly hard again absolutely happening in the present.

He opened his eyes, noting the room was still dark. Which meant at best they'd scored one or two hours of sleep. They both definitely needed more.

Laurel's hand slapped against his bare chest and he winced.

"Where?" she demanded into her phone receiver. "She's all right?" Laurel covered the receiver with one hand. "They found Lizzie," she whispered. "A little beat-up but mostly okay."

"Does Clint know?"

She shook her head, so Grady got out of bed to find his phone. It was somewhere on Laurel's side of the room so he walked around. Her floor was neat as a pin except where their discarded clothes and his tossed phone, keys and wallet dotted the hardwood.

Laurel was barking demanding questions into her phone and clearly getting at least some of the responses she wanted. Grady picked up his phone and typed a text to Clint that Lizzie had been found and was okay.

He watched Laurel as she picked up a pen and notepad from her nightstand and balanced it on her lap. The sheet covered her legs, but her upper body was completely bare, and Grady wanted nothing more than to crawl back into bed and toss her phone and notes away.

But this was her job, and he was an intuitive enough man to know she would not compromise her priorities. He wished he didn't admire that so much about her.

There was something like panic beating in his chest because he wanted… Well, for the first time in his adult life he wanted something that was out of his control. He could fight for his name, for Rightful Claim, for Bent, but what lay before him with this woman wasn't a fight.

It would be something like a give-and-take, and sometimes he wondered if deep down inside he was just his parents—all take.

But he wasn't a coward. Wouldn't allow himself to be. Panic didn't rule him, and neither did fear. If he wanted to give and take, he damn well would.

Laurel finished writing something down, then clicked off her phone and set it neatly on the nightstand.

"They haven't found who took her. Apparently she was dumped back at the same gas station she was taken from. She doesn't have a description, but they did find that the license plate Lizzie had written down in her room was a Nebraska plate, and Nebraska plates are yellow, which means the plate we have and the car that took her are probably one and the same."

"You think this is all the work of one man?"

"I'm not sure. But one man has the answers and I need to find them. Apparently Lizzie knew her father was in trouble and had been doing her own poking around—mostly with the help of Clint. She's been pretty tight-lipped about what happened while she was kidnapped, so I'm going to go question her. Maybe she'll feel more comfortable with a woman." Laurel was already out of bed, pulling on a T-shirt.

Belatedly she noticed it was his. She shook her head and moved to take it off again, but he stopped her, putting a hand to her abdomen.

"And if she gives you a tip-off to who did this? What are you going to do?"

She looked up at him, then blinked as if to focus herself. Her gaze slid down his naked body, which he had to say he didn't mind.

She shook her head as if to clear it. "I'll follow procedure to bring whoever it is in for questioning. We both need to get dressed and I'll drop you off at the Carson Ranch."

Grady bit back all the jumbled worry inside of him. It had only been a few days of working side by side with her, and she'd been a cop for a long time, but he didn't like… Well, the idea of not being there when she went up against a man capable of murder.

"I need to check on things at the bar," he forced himself to say. "When Vanessa runs things, I tend to find myself a mess. Drop me off there."

She chewed on her bottom lip for a second before reaching out and touching his bare chest. "Just because we have a lead doesn't mean you're not still in danger. You should be somewhere protected, and with people."

"You're in danger all the time. Just by being a cop, right?" he said quietly, because he knew it was true. He *knew* that. He understood that. He just wanted her to understand… Something.

She absorbed those words, seeming to take in their weight. She didn't brush that statement off, she considered it. Which meant something, maybe something more than it should.

It was another layer. They didn't necessarily have to talk every step through for them to understand each other.

"There is a slight difference," she said carefully.

"Rationally, I get that."

"And irrationally?"

"Irrationally, I want you by my side always so I can know you're safe. *I* want to keep *you* safe."

She stared up at him, her fingertips on his chest, and it was like a moor to this world. She was his anchor to this world. This Delaney cop. Somehow it made all the sense. Because she was the last thing he should ever want, of course she was the only one who fit.

She got up on her tiptoes and brushed her mouth across his. "I don't…" She took a deep breath and squared her shoulders, all the while looking him in the eye. "I don't want last night to be a one-time thing."

"Good, because it's not," he returned gruffly.

"And I don't just mean the sex."

"I know what you mean."

"You feel the same way?" she asked him directly, so brave and certain and good.

It grated somehow, because he wasn't all that good, and she probably deserved someone better, but he'd be damned if he let her have another man. He took her mouth with his, the opposite of her sweet little peck. He kissed her long and hard and hot. "You are mine, Laurel Delaney. End of story."

Her mouth curved, almost as if she was indulging him. "And you are mine, Grady Carson." She patted his chest. "I'm surprised you're not being a baby about it."

"Maybe once I've had a good night's sleep I'll work up a good tantrum."

She smiled at him, but it didn't ease this feeling inside of him. Separate from all the being each other's.

"I don't think we should separate right now," he said, even knowing it was a losing battle to go against what she needed to do.

"I need to question Lizzie alone, and I need a few hours to concentrate. Besides, they let Lizzie go of their own volition. Things are de-escalating. There might still be danger out there, but I think it's weakened. Besides, you have work to do as much as me. You know it."

Grady grunted, irritated she was right. "Something doesn't feel right. Just like the other night when Clint didn't show up. Something doesn't… Something isn't adding up."

"I agree. That's why I need a few hours at the station. Talk to Lizzie. Look at some documents Hart found. I need my concentration on this case for a good two hours. And I can't do that with you around."

"You flatter me, princess."

"Get dressed. I'll drop you off at Rightful Claim, as long as someone can be there with you. I don't want you being alone. I'll put in my few hours at the station, and then..." She chewed on her bottom lip again.

"And then what?"

She trailed the fingertips over his beard. "I'll come and find you."

"You had better." He kissed her, meaning for it to be soft, subtle, just to prove he could. But it evolved somehow, as it always did with her. Wildfire and need. "We both need showers before we go, don't you think?"

"We are not both going to fit in my shower," she said with a breathless laugh.

"But we could give it the old college try," he returned, tugging her toward a door that had to lead to the bathroom. And when she went with him willingly, laughing and naked, he figured things might just be all right after all.

Chapter Sixteen

Laurel drove toward the Bent County Sheriff's Department after dropping Grady off at Rightful Claim, not exactly feeling rested. She was still tired, because she'd grabbed maybe just three hours of sleep. But it had been good, heavy sleep. And something like giddiness was keeping her going.

She was a little embarrassed at that. How much excitement and drive this whole Grady thing had given her. She should calm down. She should be rational.

She and Grady were in some very odd circumstances and it was likely causing heightened feelings…or something. The reality of themselves was possibly a little different outside of the bedroom.

Which was all her fear talking, actually. Because last night and this morning had been good. The kind of good that was overwhelming. The kind of good you had to work for and sacrifice things for. In equal-ish measure.

She blew out a breath. She didn't have time to really work through all that. She had to question Lizzie, and see if the ballistics report had come back yet. Her focus had to be the job, and then she could figure out her personal life.

Because that was the priority list of her life. Always had been.

Why did it suddenly feel like a weight?

She shook her head, focusing on the sun rising behind her. Which was when she realized the same car had been following her for a while now. The same kind of car Clint had mentioned when describing the man who'd taken Lizzie.

The car was far back enough she couldn't make out the letters and numbers on the plate, but she could tell it was yellowish. Just as Clint had described.

She inhaled, then slowly breathed out through her mouth, focusing on being calm and following procedure.

What if they've been following you since before you left Rightful Claim? What if someone is following Grady?

She couldn't focus on *that*. She had to focus on what to do in her here and now. Because she'd left Bent city limits, and the sun was only just beginning to rise. The highway out of town was deserted, and the current stretch she was on was at a high enough elevation that the shoulder was mostly guardrail to prevent cars from going off the slight rocky cliff.

Taking a glance in her rearview mirror as often as she could, she grabbed for her radio without looking at it.

"Dispatch. 549. Rush traffic," she said as calmly as she could manage.

"Go ahead 549."

Before she could get the next words out of her mouth, an engine roared close—too close. She flicked a glance in the rearview mirror just in time to see the black car plow into the back of hers.

She jerked forward, her face smashing into the airbag as she felt her car skid forward and then sideways, metal screeching against the guardrail. That noise reminded her of how precarious her situation was. Because if this car succeeded in pushing her over it, she'd be tumbling down a pretty steep, rocky drop.

She ignored the pain in her head and focused

on her grip on the wheel. She jerked it as far to the right as the airbag would allow, braking as hard as she could while she did so.

She had to get out of the car. While it offered some protection, she could be more agile on foot. And possibly run down the steep ravine without plunging to her death.

She couldn't see anything with the airbag in her vision, but the screeching of the guardrail had stopped and so had her movement. She imagined the attacker was reversing to plow into her again, so she had to act fast.

She pushed hard, opening the door open and scrambling out of the car as she disentangled herself from the airbag and seat belt. She grabbed her gun out of her belt as she looked around, trying to find the other car.

It had indeed reversed and was now speeding toward her. Laurel didn't have time to think twice—she ran and jumped over the guardrail, half running, half stumbling down the rocky hillside.

If she drew him into a chase, she could shoot him. Of course, he likely had a gun himself, but at least she'd have a chance to fight back. She glanced behind her—nothing but rocks and bent guardrail.

She surveyed the landscape in front of her. It was mostly open, though there were a few swells of land she might be able to hide behind with enough of a head start.

The biggest problem was she didn't have her radio or her cell. All she had was her gun. So, she kept running, checking over her shoulder every few minutes for signs of someone following her.

She was maybe halfway to a decent cover of rocks and swell of land when a figure appeared, stepping over the guardrail. He was wearing all black, including a ski mask, just as Clint had described the man who'd taken Lizzie.

Well, he was not going to take her. She raised her gun, tried to aim, only to realize her vision wasn't clear. Blood was dripping down into her eyes. Blood? Where had that come from?

She tried to blink it away, finally becoming cognizant of the fact her head was throbbing and burning. In the adrenaline of the moment, she hadn't realized she'd been hurt, but some of that reality was getting through to her now. The world tilted, but she breathed through it and fired off a shot in the direction of the man in black.

She didn't even try to see if she'd hit her target. She started running again, trying to figure out where she was. If there was somewhere she could go. She was injured and isolated, but she wasn't outnumbered, probably, and just because she was hurt didn't mean she was witless.

After another scan of the area, and remembering where she'd been on the road, she realized she was close to the back entrance to the Carson Ranch she'd dropped Grady off at the other day.

She didn't want to lead this man to the Carsons, but she didn't have a choice. She needed a phone. She needed help. If she at least got to the property, she might get hurt, but maybe someone would find her before she was killed. Maybe.

A shot rang out and she winced at how close it sounded, but nothing touched her. Still, it was too close for comfort, and proof the man was armed with a deadly weapon.

Lungs burning, everything in her body a painful, aching throb, Laurel tried to pull up her shirt and wipe away the blood that was impeding her vision as she ran.

But even without blood in her eyes, her vision was getting blurrier. She felt dizzy and sick but she knew she had to keep running. Someone was after her. The man who'd killed Jason, who'd kidnapped Lizzie. It had to be him.

She got to the back entrance of the Carson Ranch without the man catching up to her or firing off another short. She just had to get to the house, or maybe Noah would be out somewhere close working. Someone who would hear something, do something. She had to hope and pray for that, because she knew her time was running out.

Her legs buckled and the world around her was suddenly dark instead of the picturesque fall morning. She didn't quite realize she'd fallen until her shoulder hit the hard ground.

She tried to get up, but her body wasn't listening to her mind. She could hear approaching footsteps closing in on her.

Dimly she hoped Grady was okay and at Rightful Claim, working and giving Vanessa a hard time. She swallowed at the nausea threatening, praying she'd left enough clues and wreckage for whoever found her to figure out who this man was and where he'd come from.

Somewhat belatedly, she realized she still had her hand on her gun. The gun. She placed her finger on the trigger and when it sounded like the man was right on top of her, she managed to roll onto her back and shoot.

GRADY FROWNED AT his phone with growing irritation. He'd been patient all morning and not called Laurel to see what was going on. But it was nearly two o'clock and there'd been no word from her. Not to him. Not to Clint.

Grady tried to convince himself she'd found a lead and was following it. He tried to convince himself she was doing her job. If something had happened, wouldn't he have heard something? If not from Laurel herself, from *someone*.

Then again, why would anyone think to tell him about the goings-on of Laurel Delaney?

When Dylan Delaney stormed into the bar before they'd officially opened for the day, everything in Grady went cold and still.

The Delaneys did not come into his bar.

"Where is she? What have you gotten her messed up with?"

Grady stood behind the bar, willing his temper to behave. He'd never cared for Laurel's brother the slick, arrogant banker who only'd ever looked down at any Carson in his bank. But Dylan *was* her brother, and maybe he knew something that Grady didn't. It'd grate more if he wasn't so worried.

"What do *I* have your *cop* sister mixed up in?"

"She might be a cop, and this might have more to do with the case she's working on, but when Carson property is involved, so are you. I know it."

"What are you talking about?" Grady demanded, keeping himself unnaturally still. He couldn't *react* yet. First he needed facts.

"My sister disappeared. They've traced footsteps and blood to *your* property, and there's a lot of talk about how you left the station with her last night. So I want to know what you did to her."

Grady pushed out from behind the bar, ignoring Dylan's demands. He pulled his phone out and dialed the ranch. No answer. He dialed Noah's cell, which went straight to voice mail. Ty was in the back, and if he'd heard anything, he would've told Grady by now.

"Ty," Grady called, already to the door. "Lock up. Meet me at the ranch." He didn't wait to see if his cousin would listen. He called Vanessa. Nothing.

He took his keys out of his pocket as he swung out the front doors.

"You don't walk away from me, Carson," Dylan threatened, hot on his heels.

"I'll fight you after your sister's been found, if that's what you're gunning for. But I've got more important things to do right now than deal with you." He got on his motorcycle.

"I'm following you," Dylan shouted over the roar of the motorcycle's engine, as if that was some kind of deterrent. Grady didn't even respond.

He took off, breaking every possible traffic law to get to the ranch. There was a cop car parked at the front of the house, but he didn't see anyone in it. He scanned the land, heartbeat thumping painfully in his chest.

Blood. Blood. She was bleeding somewhere, and he couldn't do a thing about it.

Except she'd gotten here. His property. There had to be something he could do. Had to be.

Dylan's car pulled up next to him, windows

down. "I don't know what you think you're going to do."

"I'm going to find her," Grady replied. Some way. Somehow. There was nothing else *to* do.

"Why are *you* going to do anything? The police are searching for her, and if you had anything to do with—"

"I don't have anything to do with it. I love her." Which was not exactly a *surprise* admission, just an uncomfortable one.

"That's… You're a *Carson*."

"Yeah, I'll worry about that some other time." He scanned the area again, trying to figure out where to start. He had to stop jabbering with Dylan and actually think. Formulate a plan.

"They're at the back entrance," Dylan offered. "What's the quickest way?"

Grady frowned at the sleek sports vehicle Laurel's brother drove. "That car isn't going to make it over this hard terrain."

"It will," Dylan said, everything about him severe and determined. "Now, what's the quickest way?"

"Follow me." Grady took off, narrowly missing wrecking out when he went over a swell of land too fast, but it didn't matter. Nothing mattered aside from finding Laurel.

When they reached the back entrance, there was a whole area taped off with caution tape. The deputy who'd searched the Adams's house with Laurel the other day frowned in his direction as Grady swung off the motorcycle and stormed toward the tape.

"You're going to have to stay back," Hart said firmly.

Grady only did so because he knew the guy was trying to do his job. He glanced at the crowd. Three deputies. And Noah.

He went to stand next to his cousin. "Tell me what you know."

"No signs of a vehicle," Noah said. "But Laurel's car was found crashed into a guardrail on the highway. Someone rear-ended her, but the car that caused the accident is nowhere to be found. The cops found a trail of blood that led here."

"That's a mile at least."

Noah nodded grimly. "Vanessa's with Clint and another officer at the house. I've offered to search the higher elevations on my horse, but they're still making a decision."

"Screw that." Grady looked at Noah's horse

tied to a tree, placidly standing a few yards off. "I'm going."

"There's the old stone church up on the ridge. It's the only kind of place to hide anywhere near here," Noah said quietly, angling them away from the deputies gathering evidence and talking earnestly. "Unless someone picked her up on the road, but the cops don't think so. I told them about the church, but—"

Grady shook his head. "They've got their procedure, but we don't. I'm not waiting around. I'm going to take your horse up there. You and Delaney go back and get more horses, rifles, whatever you can. We search for her ourselves."

Noah looked suspiciously at Dylan. "You really want to take him?"

"I'm her brother," Dylan interjected. "Finding Laurel is all that matters."

Noah nodded at that. "All right."

"Wait until I'm gone, then take my bike. It'll be quickest to get back to the barn." Grady handed Noah the keys. "I'm going to ride Star right up the property line to the stone church. You cut up from the barn the opposite direction. Got your cell?"

Noah nodded.

"You see anything, anything comes up, call. I'll do the same. Something big happens, 911, cops, whatever. The only important thing is finding her safe, and keeping yourself out of harm's way. Got it?"

"What about keeping *your*self safe?"

Grady didn't bother to lie. "I'll do what I have to do. Whatever it takes."

"Grady—"

But he was done arguing and standing around. He strode over to Noah's horse and untied the reins from the tree. He mounted Star and gave her neck a quick pat before leading her away from the group and tape.

Once he had a little space, he urged her into a trot. Straight toward the ridge that would lead him up to the old stone church that had been abandoned probably a century ago, and sat just off Carson property, owned and tended by no one.

"Hey, where are you going?" one of the deputies shouted.

Grady didn't bother to answer. He was going to find Laurel. One way or another.

Chapter Seventeen

Laurel heard voices. Unfamiliar voices. She knew she had to open her eyes, but she couldn't seem to manage it. Her head hurt, with so much pain she could barely think past it.

But there were voices, and even though everything hurt and jumbled together, something inside of her knew she had to listen to those voices.

"What kind of idiot are you? There's no way out of this. You've screwed everything up," a man's voice hissed, all restrained fury.

"We could kill her," the other voice suggested, as if he were suggesting getting dessert at a restaurant.

"*You* could kill her," the man retorted. "She did shoot you, after all. We could call it self-defense, perhaps."

"I've done all your dirty work," the second

man returned, clearly not happy about it. "All of it."

"That's what I pay you for, and this… You've made this an irreparable mess. You should do all the dirty work when you were the one to muddy it all up. A simple job."

"Simple? Kill two guys and kidnap a girl?"

"You failed at one of those, and the girl was safely returned. You're in the clear there."

The second man laughed bitterly. "I'm not doing another thing for you until I get my full compensation."

"No full compensation until we take care of this problem."

Nausea rolled through Laurel, but she tried to breathe through it. Some of the confusion in her mind cleared, even with the constant ache in her head. The fact they hadn't killed her yet meant *something.*

She had a chance. A chance to live. A chance to escape. If she could only act.

Breathe in. Breathe out. Focus.

She thought she could maybe open her eyes now, but figured it would be best if she gathered her wits before she gave any indication she was conscious. Formulate a plan. Obviously they had weapons. There were two of them, and only one of her.

She blew out a breath, willing herself not to throw up. She was sitting on the cold floor, and her arms were behind her back. Which meant they were tied together. She catalogued the rest of her body as much as she could with her eyes closed and her brain still scrambled.

There was something around her ankles as well. Something hard and cold behind her back. She was cold. So cold.

Focus.

Except she must have said that out loud, or moved, or something.

"She's conscious," the angrier man muttered.

Laurel blinked her eyes open. The man all in black was pulling his mask back down, and she missed any identifying markers. The other man wasn't anywhere she could see, but she was afraid to turn her head to fully search the room.

"Where am I?"

The man in black laughed. "Jupiter, sweetheart."

Dark eyes glittered behind the ski mask and Laurel knew without a shadow of a doubt she had to escape quickly. Even if the other man didn't want to kill her, this one did.

"I'm going to throw up."

He rolled his eyes, turning to somewhere just outside Laurel's vision. She tried to turn her head but pain pierced her skull.

"Just kill her," Angry Man was saying. "*You* this time. So we're both in this and I know you're not going to try and pawn this all off on me."

"Take her outside until she's done. Then bring her back. If we decide to kill her, we need to make sure we have everything we need first."

Angry Man grumbled, but he walked over to her. Laurel was shaking, and no amount of breathing helped that. When two rough hands grabbed her and pulled her to her feet, she swayed and closed her eyes.

He pushed her back roughly against the wall, and she leaned against it, trying to make the world stop spinning. She realized somewhat belatedly he'd untied her legs.

"Walk," he ordered gruffly.

Weaving and swaying, Laurel began to walk. She didn't make an effort to change her weakened gait. The weaker he thought she was, the better. But moving helped. Stepping outside helped.

Except for the fact nothing around her gave her any clue as to where she was. There were trees and sky and rocky ground.

"Well? You gonna throw up or not?"

Laurel bent forward. "I need my hands. I have to use the bathroom."

The man laughed harshly. "Like hell. Stop talking and start retching or we're going back in there right this second." He waved his gun in her face. "If I wasn't trying to prove a point, I would've blown your brains out hours ago."

Hours. Had it been hours? She didn't recognize this place, though it still looked like Wyoming. But maybe it wasn't. Maybe she was far away from home and help.

She bent over, pretending to gag, trying not to cry. Slowly she raised her gaze, trying to find…something. Anything. A place to run and hide. A clue as to where she was.

"You run, I'll only shoot you. Somewhere that'll take a long time to bleed out so you can die a long and terrible death."

She turned her head to look at this man. "Why?"

He shrugged. "Why not?"

Something rustled behind them and the man pushed her down. Since her hands were tied behind her, she couldn't stop the fall. She could only turn her head and brace her body for impact. The sound that came out of her when she hit the hard, cold ground was loud and involuntary.

"Shut up," Angry Man said, giving her a swift, painful kick to the leg. "And don't move."

Laurel sucked in a breath and tried not to sob as she blew it back out. She tilted her head to see where Angry Man had gone. He was slinking around the side of the building, gun held at the ready.

Laurel couldn't help but think it was a squirrel or raccoon or something. Who would stumble upon this…

She looked around her as best she could in her prone position. It was a clearing, the building behind her stone and clearly abandoned for a long time. Windows gone, any clue to what it could have been completely gone.

Except the cross at the very top of the roof.

Oh, God, she knew where she was. She and Vanessa had snuck up here once as kids and spent the night telling each other ghost stories.

One of the few times she'd been convinced breaking the rules wasn't the worst thing in the world.

That time was long past, but that church was Wyoming. It was home. She was so close to the Carson Ranch she still had a chance, a real chance, to escape. As long as Angry Man didn't shoot her first.

But he'd disappeared around the corner of the building. And yes, he could likely outrun her in her current injured and tied-up state, but maybe…

A shot rang out, jolting her. She rolled herself onto her side and managed to leverage herself up to her knees. Her vision blurred, but she pushed through it and up onto her feet. She had to… She had to…

When a figure rushed around the corner of the building, Laurel thought for sure she was hallucinating. She had to be. Maybe she'd died. Or was unconscious and dreaming.

Grady stopped short, then swore roughly. Before she could blink, he was in front of her, gingerly touching her shoulder.

"Are you all right?"

"There's another one, Grady," Laurel said, surveying the stone church. They were like sitting ducks out here, and the man inside had to have heard the gunshot.

Except in the next moment, a man was stepping out of the church. He didn't wear a mask or all black and she didn't even see a weapon on him.

"Thank God. Thank God. I was so scared," he said, moving toward her and Grady.

Grady pushed her behind him, holding his pistol up. "Don't come any closer," he ordered the man. "Hold on to me," he whispered to her.

"Please, you've got to help me," the man implored.

Laurel frowned, holding on to Grady's shirt. From everything she'd heard, this man was the leader of the whole debacle. But maybe in her jumbled head she'd been confused.

"That man you shot was holding me captive, much like you." The middle-aged man looked imploringly at her. "Thank God we're both all right."

"Laurel?" Grady asked.

It didn't feel right, but everything was so topsy-turvy and she couldn't trust what she'd heard and what she hadn't.

"The police are on their way. They can sort out whether or not that's true," Grady said firmly, his aim of the gun not wavering from the man's chest.

"Something isn't right," Laurel whispered, more to herself than to Grady.

"What isn't right?" he returned, as quietly and under-his-breath as she'd spoken.

"I don't know." She just didn't know.

GRADY WASN'T ABOUT to lower his weapon on this guy, no matter what he said. Or Laurel said, for that matter. While he wasn't dressed like the man he'd shot on the other side of the church—no mask, no weapon—he was still here. Unharmed, while Laurel's entire face was streaked with blood.

He couldn't think about that, though. If he did he might sink to his knees at the sheer pain of it. That she'd been this hurt, and was somehow still alive. Still here. He had to get her safe.

"I'd feel so much better if you put the gun down," the guy said with a nervous chuckle.

Grady didn't move. "I wouldn't."

"Then maybe I should just go back inside until the police—"

"Don't move."

Something about the guy's expression didn't

sit right with Grady. Something about this whole thing didn't sit right, and if the cops didn't get here soon, he'd be forced to act. Because he wasn't going to make Laurel stand through much more of this.

"Why don't you sit down," Grady said. When the man started to bend his knees, Grady rolled his eyes. "Not you. Her."

"Oh," Laurel breathed behind him. "I better stay standing."

"Laurel!"

If Grady wasn't mistaken, it was Dylan's voice, which meant Dylan and Noah had arrived. The cops couldn't be too far back.

"Someone call an ambulance," Grady barked. "Noah, can you ride Laurel out of here without banging her up any more?"

Noah dismounted, about five seconds after Dylan. Both men charged up the hill, taking in the scene around them.

"I'll take her myself," Dylan said hotly.

"I don't know if a horse ride would be the best thing for her in this condition," Noah said calmly. "Head injury—"

"She'll be fine. She needs a doctor fast."

"If all the men could stop posturing and listen to what *I* have to say," Laurel interjected, but she was leaning against Grady and shaking.

"I'm sorry, are any of you a police officer? Or someone who could convince this man to stop pointing his gun at me?" the man Grady hadn't taken his eyes off said.

Grady exchanged a look with Noah, but Noah didn't seem too keen on the idea, either. "How'd you get up here?" Noah asked.

The man tugged at the collar of his shirt. "I… I don't know. I was brought here against my will."

"How?" Laurel asked from behind Grady.

"W-what?" the man said.

"How did one man bring you and me here against our will?" Laurel asked, her voice sounding stronger and clearer than it had.

"I'm not sure how you arrived, but I was brought here yesterday. Now—"

"Why weren't you tied up?"

The man stood stock-still, everything about him frozen. "I…was."

"No you weren't," Laurel returned, and she moved from where she'd been leaning against Grady's back, to stand next to him. She leaned on him for support, which was certainly a concern, but she stood there, determined. "I saw you. I heard you."

The man's eyes darted around where they all stood in the clearing.

"There isn't anywhere to go," Grady said fiercely, noting that Noah and Dylan had raised their rifles to aim at the man as well.

"And even if you got out of here, I'd find you," Noah said calmly. "I can find anything in these mountains."

The man licked his lips nervously. "I… I don't know what you're all talking about. I don't… I'm a victim. And I haven't done anything wrong. If you do anything to me, I will sue you."

"And who will I sue for paying that man to run me off the road?"

"I did no such thing—" he smirked a little "—that you'll be able to prove."

"Do you own a black sedan, Nebraska license plate 85A GHX?"

The man visibly paled, and it was Grady's turn to smirk. "I think you might be on to something, Deputy," he offered cheerfully.

"I'm going to go out on a limb and say

you're employed by the company that runs Evergreen Mining."

"I don't see what that has to do with anything."

"But I do," Laurel said. "I heard your conversation with the other man, and I've got so much evidence built up. All I needed was the man behind it, and here you are."

"You can't..." He shook his head, looking around more desperately. "You're lying."

"I guess we'll find out how much when the police arrive. Noah or Dylan, will you walk around and see if you can find the car?"

"Gladly," Dylan said, sounding about as lethal as Grady felt.

The only thing that kept Grady in place was Laurel leaning against him. Otherwise he'd be more than a little tempted to beat this guy to a bloody pulp.

"You can't do this. My lawyers will have a field day with this. None of you know what you're talking about and...and... This is ludicrous. I'll take you for everything you're worth."

"That supposed to be scary?"

"You have nothing to hold me on. Nothing."

"Cops are here," Dylan called from the other

side of the stone church. "And I found the car. Just as Laurel described."

The man darted for the woods, but Grady fired his weapon, hitting him in the upper thigh. The man fell to the ground with a howl. And again, Grady would have gladly gone over and gotten a few kicks in, but Laurel was leaning, saying his name.

"Grady."

He glanced down at her. Her eyes were drooping, and underneath the awful blood all over her, her complexion was gray.

"Open your eyes, baby."

She shook her head almost imperceptibly. "Can't."

"Come on, princess. Stay with me here." He moved the arm not holding a gun around her waist, holding her up. She clutched his shirt, but it was as though her legs didn't hold her up. Her legs buckled.

"I really don't feel well."

"Laurel." But her eyes had rolled back, her body going limp. Grady looked up wildly, heart beating with panic against his chest. "Hart," he barked when the deputy came into view. "Get your car up here now."

Grady had to hand it to the young deputy—

he didn't balk at taking orders from a civilian. Hart turned and ran back down the hill, shouting orders to the other deputies with him.

Chapter Eighteen

Laurel wasn't a fan of waking up from unconsciousness not knowing where she was or what had happened. She vaguely remembered the stone church, something about the man who'd been responsible for all this.

She definitely remembered Grady. He'd held her up and kept her safe.

"Grady?" Whatever sound that came out of her mouth certainly didn't sound like his name. She cleared her raw throat and tried again. "Grady?" She tried to open her eyes but it was all too bright.

"Shh. We're right here." Jen's voice. Her sister.

"Jen. Where's Grady?"

"I can't believe she's saying that Carson's name. She must be delirious."

"Hello to you, too, Dad." She felt a large

hand on her arm. She imagined it was her father's, and despite all his blustering she was sure he was worried sick. "Can someone dim the lights."

"That should be better," another male voice said.

Laurel's eyes flew open. "Cam." Her brother closest in age to her had been deployed for a while and she hadn't seen him in over a year. But here he was, in her hospital room.

Hospital. Why was everyone here?

"Oh, God, am I dying?"

Jen took her hand. "No, but you certainly gave us all a scare. You lost a lot of blood and needed a lot of stitches. Collapsed lung, bruised ribs and a broken nose." Jen let out a shaky breath. "And Dylan said it could have been so much worse."

Laurel looked around at her family in the hospital room, and she knew she should want this and this alone. She was healing and her family was here because they loved her.

"I need to see Grady." She turned to Jen, imploringly, figuring Jen would be her best, softest-hearted bet. "Please. He saved me, you know." She looked around at her stone-faced father and an even stonier-faced Cam. "He saved me. I need to speak with him."

"I'll get him," Dylan surprised her by saying.

Dad sputtered, Jen soothed him, and Cam ushered all of them out of the room, pausing at the door to look back at her. "I didn't expect to come home and find you looking like hell, sis."

"Are you home to stay?"

"Yeah."

"I'm very glad," she said, feeling overly emotional. She'd blame that on whatever machines she was hooked up to or whatever was in the IV.

"Me, too." And then he disappeared, and only seconds later, Grady stepped in. He was big and strong and she wanted to *weep*. Because he was here, and he'd saved her. "You're here," she managed to rasp.

"Where else would I be, princess?" he asked gruffly.

"What happened?"

"You were hurt—"

"With the guy. The head guy. It's all a blur after I told him I had evidence and—"

"He made a break for it."

She squeaked in outrage.

Grady's mouth curved grimly. "I shot him."

"Oh. I don't remember that. Is he dead?"

"No. Fared better than you. Other guy's in critical. The leader of this whole thing has a million lawyers crawling all over the place, but you built a pretty tight case against the guy. Evidence all over his car that he had Lizzie. And while the other guy may have been driving the car, it's registered to the main guy. Not quite the criminal mastermind he fancied himself."

"So who was the not-head guy?"

"Hired muscle. Basically a hit man he was using however necessary to try and cover all this up."

"Was he really doing all this for EPA violations?"

Grady shrugged, still standing near the door. "We don't know. He's got enough lawyers to block every cop in America, I think."

"Why are you standing all the way over there?" she demanded.

"Because I want to touch you so bad it hurts," he said, hands jammed in his pockets, something like but not quite fury vibrating off him.

"You can touch me."

"You look terrible, princess."

"I'll heal. Come here."

Slowly, he took a step forward, and then another, until he was standing over her, looking at her face as though she'd jabbed a knife in his chest.

He put a fingertip to her collarbone, she assumed since it wasn't bruised or scraped.

"You gave me quite the scare," he murmured, his fingertip warm and gentle on her skin.

"It wasn't exactly roses and unicorns from where I stood, either."

"Laurel." He looked so grim, so serious. Like he was about to deliver the most terrible news on the face of the planet. With her actual name to boot. "I love you."

She blinked. "What?"

"You heard me," he returned grumpily, shoving his hands back in his pockets.

"But..."

"And I'm not prone to saying that, so don't expect me to repeat it."

"Grady," she reached out for him, but he stepped away from the bed.

"Oh, fine," he grumbled. "If you're going to be that way about it."

"What wa—"

"I love you," he blurted as if she'd somehow *forced* the admission out of him, and she was to blame for all of it. "I love you. Grady Carson loves Laurel Delaney. Are you happy?" He raked his fingers through his hair.

She wanted to laugh. He'd lost his mind, and he loved her. Really. "Grady."

"And don't think you're getting out of this," he said, pointing at her. "You started it. You're stuck with me now."

"Come here," she said as forcefully as she could manage. "And calm down."

He looked at her with that same desolate expression he'd used to say he loved her. "You could have died."

A lump clogged her throat, but she spoke through it. "So could you. You came in guns blazing, all by yourself."

"Hours," he said, his voice breaking just there at the end. "You were gone hours before we found you."

"Grady."

"What?" he snapped.

She cupped his face with her hands, reveling in the sharp spikes of his beard. "I love you," she said, looking directly into those beautiful blue eyes, knowing without a doubt that whatever crazy Bent feud nonsense was thrown their way, no matter how many murder investigations went awry, they would make it through together.

He kissed the spot on her collarbone he'd touched earlier. "You're darn right you do, princess."

Two weeks later

When Laurel Delaney sauntered into Rightful Claim on a snowy day, dressed in a drab Bent County PD polo and baggy khaki pants, with her badge attached to her hip, Grady Carson wondered how he'd ever thought he could fight the feeling in his gut he got every time she walked into his bar.

A century-old feud hadn't stood a chance against this wave of possession. Love. She was his. He was hers. Beginning and end of story.

"So, the doctors clear you?" he asked casually.

She slid onto a barstool. "Desk duty," she said disgustedly, some of the cuts on her face still red and a terrible reminder of that day not so long ago. "I can work in-house and lose my marbles."

"I'm guessing that's wise."

She made a rude noise. "I'm fine."

"That's not what you said last night."

She wrinkled her nose. "You just hit my ribs the wrong way. I don't plan on getting naked and sweaty with anyone I'm investigating."

"Good to hear."

"I did get some good news today," she said leaning forward on the bar, then wincing.

He winced right along with her. He thought it had been bad enough seeing her bloody and passed out, or in that horrible white hospital bed, but watching her *heal* and push herself too hard was a new pain he'd never known.

"What's that?" he asked, sliding her a Coke.

"The muscle woke up yesterday. Lawyered up, but he made a plea bargain. Looks like he's going to turn on Mr. Head Guy."

Head Guy. Aaron Zifle. The head of the mining corporations safety department, drowning in safety violations and trying to keep his pretty young wife sparkling in diamonds. Apparently he'd been about to lose his job and so desperate to keep the well-paying position he'd decided the only way to deal with Jason Delaney's accusation had been to kill.

At least that was Laurel's theory after her

nonstop investigating while she'd still been forced to spend most of her days in bed. Grady was inclined to believe her since he spent most of his days at her bedside, listening to her chatter.

Vanessa had nearly run his bar into the ground, at least in his estimation, but it still stood, and he was back to work, and Laurel was trying to be.

"That is good news. Make his trial airtight, won't it?"

"Yes. They'll likely up his bond with that information, too. The chances of him getting out of what he's done, even with his team of lawyers, is pretty slim."

"We should celebrate."

"How?" She rubbed at her rib. "I'm not sure I'm up for any serious celebrating."

"How about this. After I close up, I pack all my things up and move them to your cabin."

Her eyebrows furrowed together. "Move. Into my cabin. You?"

"Yes, I believe that's what I meant."

"But… We… We've barely dated," she said, her eyebrows furrowing deeper.

"True."

"My family… A Carson living on Delaney land? The town might have us tarred and feathered."

"Could be."

"And the bar." She gestured around to encompass all of Rightful Claim. "Don't you have to be here at all hours?"

"Not *all* hours. I was thinking about giving Vanessa more control, and the apartment—she's been angling for it for months."

Laurel blinked at him, beautiful and strong and absolutely everything he wanted to wake up to. Go to bed with. Build a life with.

"This is crazy," she said, shaking her head.

But she hadn't said no, and he knew her well enough. "Absolutely insane. So, what do you say?"

Her face broke out into a grin. "How soon can you close up?"

When he leaned across the bar and gave her a nice, hard kiss, a few cheers went up around them. A few mutters. One boo he was pretty sure came from Ty.

But Grady Carson didn't care much, because Laurel Delaney was his. Like it was always meant to be.

* * * * *